GIRL CRUSH

GIRL CRUSH
WOMEN'S EROTIC FANTASIES

EDITED BY
R. GAY

Published in the United States, by Cleis Press Inc., 2246 Sixth St., Berkeley, California 94710.

Printed in the United States.
Cover design: Scott Idleman
Cover photograph: Image Source
Text design: Frank Wiedemann
Cleis logo art: Juana Alicia
First Edition.
10 9 8 7 6 5 4 3 2 1

ISBN: 978-1-57344-394-4

For all my girl crushes,
and for xtx

Contents

ix   *Introduction*

1   *Great Lengths* • RACHEL KRAMER BUSSEL
9   *Mirador* • TERESA LAMAI
21   *Craving Madeline* • SHANNA GERMAIN
31   *Call Me Cleopatra* • GABRIELLE FOSTER
44   *Skinny-Dipping* • ANGELA CAPERTON
57   *The Things I Can Do for Her* • DAVID ERLEWINE
65   *I Told a Stranger All About You Yesterday* • VANESSA VAUGHN
70   *Cut and Dry* • HEIDI CHAMPA
80   *Cecily* • KRIS ADAMS
94   *The Leopard-Print Menace* • MELISSA GIRA GRANT
98   *The Bachelorette* • JULIA PETERS
108   *The Girl in the Gorilla Suit* • LORI SELKE
116   *The Out-of-Towner* • DELILAH DEVLIN
129   *Rebel Girl* • KIRSTY LOGAN
136   *The Best Kind of Revenge* • GENEVA KING
147   *One Eighty* • CARRIE CANNON
157   *Running Away and Running Home Again* • ANNABETH LEONG
170   *An Introduction* • G. G. ROYALE
179   *Seduction by Proxy* • EVAN MORA
188   *Discovering Donnie* • CHEYENNE BLUE
199   *Good Neighbors* • JENNIFER GENEVA
205   *Girl Crazy* • GINA DE VRIES
213   *Psychology 101* • R. GAY

221   *About the Authors*
226   *About the Editor*

| INTRODUCTION

There is something irresistible about a crush, about wanting someone you can't have, seeing someone you can't touch; about unrequited desire and how it quickly grows into a steady burn under your skin. There is something very satisfying about a crush, about *possibility*, because really, that's what a crush is—the tender hope that the object of your affection will notice you, look your way or brush your hand; that the object of your affection will show up at your door, pull you into a passionate embrace and confess that your feelings are entirely mutual.

Girl crushes are all the rage these days as women, gay, straight or somewhere in between indulge their fantasies about female celebrities or the coworker in the next cubicle or the best friend who has always been just within yet beyond reach. A girl crush isn't any one thing—it's the admiration of a bright woman's intellect or the whimsical fantasy of kissing a beautiful movie star or the intense appreciation for a famous tennis player's perfect serve and her finely sculpted arm.

I have all kinds of girl crushes. Some are as predictable as my crush on Angelina Jolie, a goddess among mortals with her sharp facial structure, irreverent attitude and generosity, while other crushes are far more personal and pressing, like the ridiculous crush I harbor for a writer friend of mine who is by far the sexiest, most interesting and mysterious woman I know. She's that girl I want but can't have, who I look at but can't touch, who leaves me with a steady burn under my skin.

I received hundreds of submissions for this anthology and in each story, the writer detailed a different kind of girl crush. All of these writers dared to answer the question any woman who indulges in a girl crush asks—what if I could look and touch? What if I could want and have?

The twenty-three writers who contributed to this anthology boldly take up these questions with intriguing stories that are sexy and sweet and savage and more. In "The Things I Can Do for Her," David Erlewine tells the story of a young law firm associate at the sexually sadistic mercy of a demanding yet alluring partner who is insatiable in every possible way. "The Best Kind of Revenge," by Geneva King, shows us how Jana, who handles maintenance for her apartment complex, cannot resist the urge to invade the privacy of beautiful women for whom she handles repairs, until one day she gets far more than she bargained for.

G. G. Royale offers us "An Introduction," in which a young woman previously destined for an arranged marriage surrenders her inhibitions, her body and her passion to a domme in a bondage club—and in surrendering finds the strength to finally choose what she wants for herself. In a darker turn, Teresa Lamai's hard-edged and bittersweet "Mirador" is all about a fast and dirty revenge fuck in a bar bathroom between a woman and her ex-boyfriend's new lover. Expert eroticist Rachel Kramer Bussel writes of the bittersweet end to a girl crush as she realizes that sometimes unrequited passion holds more promise than satisfied desire. "I didn't want her the way I once had. I didn't want to bottom to her, and though my pussy could still feel what she'd done to me, and I remembered how good it had felt to give myself to her, my crush was over."

Two best friends, soon to be torn apart by a husband's transfer, indulge long-harbored desires in Kris Adams's "Cecily." In the midst of her passion, Mary tries to cope with the imminent separation from the woman she loves most, "She'd drink Cecily down, every last drop of her, flesh and blood, until she'd possessed her entirely, and Cliff couldn't take her away." Not all the stories in *Girl Crush* are so intense. In Jennifer Geneva's "Good Neighbors," a woman's hot, late-night encounter with the sexy couple across the street is exactly what she needs to help her through a recent breakup, and in Cheyenne Blue's tender "Discovering Donnie," though things might not always be what they seem, where love is concerned, the heart is always true.

No matter how the women in these twenty-three stories navigate the passion and promise of their girl crushes, their stories fully engage all of our senses. This collection shows us what it might be like to surrender to our girl crushes and cool the burn beneath our skin.

R. Gay

GREAT LENGTHS

Rachel Kramer Bussel

She had red hair—and by red, I mean flame orange, bold and in your face, with traces of yellow at the tips, piles and piles of long red hair, gleaming down her back, around her shoulders, matching her freckles, the perfect complement to the hoop sticking out of her eyebrow. It was the first thing anyone noticed about her, and what made my eyes linger. I don't even know what her natural hair color was, but this striking, in-your-face red suited her personality. While I somehow ended up with mousy brown hair even when I got it professionally dyed, Laura was all fiery, flaming hotness.

Laura seemed to me then to be everything I wasn't. She was bold and brash; she'd been around. We met through a mutual friend, but instantly, we were the ones who were BFFs, bonding in the way that I never seemed to with boyfriends. I worshipped her, from afar and up close. I felt like the same gawky, awkward girl I'd been in high school next to her, but she also made me feel special, like I wasn't really nerdy at all, like I was magically cool just by being graced with her presence.

Ours became the kind of friendship where you don't need a reason to see each other; in fact, you'd need a reason not to hang out. She posed me in her studio, making me feel gorgeous as her camera zoomed in on my face, red glasses and shy, beaming smile. She twirled around in long, flowing skirts and drank stiff drinks that were far beyond my limited cosmopolitan world. We stayed out all night, even on weeknights, cuddling up at dive bars in Brooklyn, eating vegetables from her garden. She made me edamame and showed me the art projects she was doing. I sat there and soaked in everything about her. She was so cool, it took me a little while to realize I was falling for her, hard, but once I knew, I knew. She wasn't just my new BFF, and I didn't just want to soak up her glamour; I wanted to kiss her, touch her, feel her hair on my breasts, feel her eyebrow ring against my thigh. I wanted to part her legs and taste her, have her draped across my lap and spank her.

We lived four blocks apart, yet we quickly became insepa-rable. I'd drop everything to hang out with her. Adventure seemed to find us, whether backstage at a show talking to Slim Moon or eating some bizarre homemade concoction at six a.m. while watching the Spice channel at a stranger's house. I didn't mind making do on two hours' sleep because Laura's energy fed my own. She was the epitome of, "I'll sleep when I'm dead," staying up late into the night to get her Final Cut Pro just right. I was just starting to figure out how to be a writer, and that writing is a kind of art, too, whereas she seemed to have the whole working artist thing down cold, never a worry, never a doubt. I felt so square, so timid next to her, which only made me want her more.

She was the kind of girl I'd have put photos of in my notebook in high school, before I knew I could worship girls from near as well as from afar, before I knew I didn't have to try to be like the girls I admired, but could simply like them, or, in this case, lust after them. Looking back, I could see I'd had girl crushes before, back before you could look someone up online, when you had to make do with moments and memories. Her being straight didn't stop me from thinking we'd be a good match; I'd bedded enough straight girls to know that. Yet as much as we said almost everything to each other, I couldn't say the most simple thing of all: I like you. I want you.

So instead, I said it to other people: her landlord, her roommate. I befriended them because they came with her seal of approval, because I thought maybe if they liked me, so would she. I did more than that, cozying up to them and even sleeping with them, but the details have become blurred, paling next to memories of what I didn't get to do with her. I'd never have gone that far with them if it hadn't been for Laura, and ultimately, I never told her about these dalliances, fearing I'd overstepped my bounds and that if she knew, it would nix any chances of me getting that close to her.

I did everything I could to take our friendship to the next level. We'd play what I call the Naked Girl Game, that video game where you reenact an adult version of a youthful memory, with scantily clad hot chicks whose bikinis you have to keep track of. The truth is, you can find hotter girls surrounding you in most any bar—the girls' look in the game is sort of '80s hair metal video—but it's still fun, and having her wedge in next to me to play it, both of us ogling girls on a screen while I thrilled to the warmth of her skin against mine, was exciting. If I'd turned just a little, I'd have been surrounded by all that glorious hair, the hair I wanted to drape all over me, bury myself in. Instead I snuggled up to her, hoping that someone would catch a glimpse of us and think we were together. I didn't care if guys hit on us, because we were a team, and I'd have gladly let any of them have her if it meant I could too. Things didn't work out like that.

Once, on her bed, I saw a book about BDSM. I wanted to ask about it, but I didn't get up the courage. Of course, it was one I also owned, one I'd practically memorized, but she didn't seem so much the type to read about sex as the type to simply do it. And then after a while she got busy with work, pulling all-nighters, and I started dating someone else, and we drifted apart the way people in fast friendships sometimes do. It became normal to go a week without hearing from her, and when she told me she was moving to L.A., I wasn't surprised. Her love affair with New York, and the imaginary one with me, was over.

It wasn't until after she moved, and I happened to be in L.A., that we finally hooked up. It's a bit fuzzy, so part of me thinks I imagined it (this is before blogging became du jour, so I can't go back and check), but I'm pretty sure it happened. By then I was a little more over her, a by-product of not seeing or talking to her every day. I'd been weaned off her earlier, but this separation felt more real, more permanent. She had moved on in some way and was less Brooklyn trailblazer than Hollywood wannabe. I couldn't relate as much as before, but I still loved hearing her talk as we cozied up over chocolate martinis and sushi at some trendy L.A. restaurant overlooking the city. The drinks would've gotten me warm no matter what, but so did she; she still had that glow that made me want to curl up next to her and have her whisper in my ear. I wasn't sure if I wanted her to drape all that hair over my body or if I wanted to grip it in my hand and pull hard, see her cool calm exterior disappear into one far more frantic and needy.

I was heading back to my friend's place, but when we went outside to say good-bye, I couldn't just give up, not this time. I turned my head and kissed her, a deep, intense kiss full of all those nights of wanting to and holding back, of kissing substitutes instead of the real thing. "I've been wanting to do that for a long time," I told her, letting down the guard I'd had up since I first started to fantasize about her. Even more than with guys, I've learned that you can't just up and confess to having a crush on a girl unless you want things to unravel before they've even started. Playing it cool was the name of the game, especially because she was straight, or at least closer to straight than I was, and I didn't want to seem predatory.

"Me too," she said, before pulling me back in for another kiss. We grappled there outside the restaurant, each of us melting into the other before gripping each other's shoulder harder, shoving our tongues in deeper, taking control. I remembered her telling me about bending over for a spanking at Burning Man, the stinging slap of leather against her ass, and how she'd liked it, but not so hard, not so fast. "Maybe I'm the one who's supposed to be holding the whip," she'd said, inspiring endless fantasies. Right now, I didn't know who would be holding what, only that I had to have her. I hadn't come all that way or waited so long to have her slink away yet again.

"Let's go back to your place," I said, trailing my hand gently over her breast, pleased to find her nipple hard and ready for me.

"No," she said, laughing when I looked at her with just a hint of the annoyance I felt on my face. "I have something better than my place," she said, grazing my cheek with a kiss when I relaxed. I didn't care where we went as long as I got to see and taste and touch all of her. I grabbed her hair, threading my fingers through it as I'd longed to do, not wanting to let go.

I don't know exactly where she took me. I wasn't blindfolded, I just didn't care. I was with her, and that was what counted. We were in the woods somewhere, not far from the road, near a hiking trail. There was a bench, and it was dark and quiet. That's where she wanted to fuck me. She pushed me down to my knees in front of her. My pussy almost hurt, that's how turned on I was. All my fantasies seemed to have culminated in that moment, and she didn't disappoint me. We were doing something exotic, far better than our brief flirtatious moments or sex with other girls. This was headier, momentous, I could tell. She pressed her short nails into the back of my neck and covered my face with her hair. "What do you want, Rachel?" she asked.

Then she lightly slapped my face. I wasn't expecting that; she doesn't really look like a domme, or what I think a domme would look like. I whimpered, because I wasn't expecting to like it so much. Now I'm a totally kinky, slutty brat, but I wasn't then, not yet. I didn't know that the tears that sprang to my eyes were only the beginning.

She leaned down and bit my lip, then ordered me to strip. I started to pull my clothes off, but she stopped me. "No. Strip for me. Tease me. Do a dance." She knew I wasn't exactly a coordinated dancer from our limited forays into clubs, and maybe that's why she requested it. I was wearing heels, at least, and I tried to pretend we were in a club, or at least a room with music, grateful I'd worn my new green silky underwear that draped across my ass in a way that made me feel like I had the hottest ass in the world. I shut my eyes, enjoying the air as it brushed against me when I took off my top, followed by my bra. "That's it," she murmured, encouraging me until I was dancing for her wearing only my glasses, nipple piercing, and heels. "Something new," she murmured as she tugged at the ring, then pulled me closer.

I sank into her lap as gracefully as I could, a little disappointed that I wasn't getting to bury my face in her pussy the way I'd dreamed of doing. I'd really never imagined she'd be topping me, taking control, touching me. I'd pegged her as straight; kinky, perhaps, but clueless about girl-on-girl lust. But when her hand found my pussy, I realized Laura wasn't clueless at all. That hand had done more than simply jerk her off to orgasm; I could tell. Her fingers sought out my wetness, then plunged inside and curved, knuckles twisting against the spot that made my face contort, her thumb zeroing in on my clit and toying with it. Maybe I looked shocked, or just overwhelmed, because she started talking again. "I bet you didn't think I knew how to do this. Oh, how little you know about me. I've been with girls, plenty of them. I just wasn't sure about us. I didn't want it to happen and then change our relationship. Plus I wanted to see how far you'd go, whether you'd let me fuck you in public where anyone could watch." I breathed heavily, dropping my head, letting her words wash over and around and through me. How could she have known how badly I wanted her and ignored my desire?

I could've been angry, but what she was doing felt too good. So what if she'd led me on? So what if I wasn't going to have some big deflowering moment? She was her own kind of top, her own kind of dyke, and as always I was just following in her wake. She pressed another finger inside me and I bit my lip, part of me wanting to tell her to stop. Was she going to fist me right here, like this? She wrapped her lips around my other nipple and tugged at it with her teeth while slowly working that fourth finger in. Laura was nothing if not full of surprises. "I bet you wanted to see my pussy, taste me, hear me coo and moan and tell you how I never thought it could be like this." She laughed then, and when I started to as well, she rearranged her hand so her thumb was right there at the doorway of my cunt. "I don't have any lube on me," she said, her voice husky now, "so you're gonna have to help me."

Real tears sprang to my eyes as I straddled her fist, a position I'd never been in before. I couldn't even remember the last time a girl had done that to me, and then it hit me: I was so used to pursuing straight girls, or ones who were "curious," that I was always in charge, even if it was all very vanilla and sweet and gooey. I was the one doing them, not getting done. But Laura had flipped the script, had gotten under my skin, had twisted me all around with a wink of her kohl-rimmed eye, a toss of her fiery locks. I looked up at her, the moonlight glowing against her still-flaming hair as it surrounded her. I came with her green eyes on me, a smile on her face part triumphant, part tender.

I never did get to go down on her. She took me home and we slept entwined together, her in panties that said, BITE ME. What a tease. She made me oatmeal in the morning and even though she was still as stunning as ever, something had changed. I didn't want her the way I once had. I didn't want to bottom to her, and though my pussy could still feel what she'd done to me, and I remembered how good it had felt to give myself to her, my crush was over. I still wanted to be her friend, but what had once seemed like the most magical thing to ever happen to me, getting to be close to her, now seemed like a dream. She seemed calm, the vibe more pajama party than fuck buddy. We hugged good-bye, but that was it: no sweet sorrow, just a hug.

At the airport, I spotted a girl reading a book by Banana Yoshimoto. She had jet black hair and a T-shirt tight enough for me to see her nipples. She was eating an ice-cream cone, lick by tantalizing lick. I sat near her, trying not to stare, and failing. She looked nothing like Laura, or any of my exes, but she had a quality that drew me to her, sassy and sexy and cute all rolled into one. One crush had ended, but a new one had begun. I made sure I sat next to her on the plane.

MIRADOR

Teresa Lamai

I don't bother turning away when I light my third cigarette. By now I almost want them to see me, or at least suspect that someone's out here, watching.

It was surprisingly easy to get up on the warehouse roof. The rusty nitrogen tank has a nice little ladder. I can see downtown Portland from here, sparkling scarlet and sugary white across the river. The moss-scented mist settles, fine as cobwebs, over my cheeks, my hair.

I lean back and watch my old apartment.

The window glows, poppy-bright in the wet darkness. The front room is exactly the same, amps and mixing boards stacked to the ceiling. Jed sits at the tableau's center, guitar in his lap. His black eyes are trained on the music stand, his brow furrowed. He's let his hair grow out, and it's wavier, glossier, almost long enough for a ponytail.

Fuck it. I should know by now that I'm going to cry every time I look at him. The stinging starts in my eyes and then fills my head.

My friends keep telling me how much happier I am without him. I haven't eaten in days. I live on coffee, cold air, and the anxious thrum of waiting, watching. I couldn't tell you what I'm looking for; I just find myself here every night. My life has shrunk around this bright, oblique conviction that if I wait long enough, if I watch hard enough, these barriers of glass and time will dissolve and I'll be back inside.

I light another cigarette and Jed looks up. I freeze.

Behind him, the bathroom door opens.

The scene looks so familiar that I almost expect it to be me coming out of the shower. But I never got Jed so excited—his eyes widen, his feet twitch. He turns toward the bathroom, his mouth slack with pure delight, as if he were watching a cake come out of the oven.

He was sitting just like that the night I first saw Christine.

I was coming from rehearsal, my legs numb. I was in the corps of *Sleeping Beauty* that season, and we'd rehearsed the wedding scene for three solid hours. My shoulders burned from holding that bow of plastic flowers over my head.

A mean, icy rain came with nightfall. I'd decided to call in sick to work. The thought of standing for another eight hours, smiling and serving cocktails, made me want to cry.

I knew I'd made the right decision when I heard Jed's music echoing through the hallways of our building. I held my breath as I eased our door open.

Jed sat naked in the candlelight, cradling his red-lacquered Spanish guitar in his lap. His head rested against the dingy wall. He sang with his eyes closed, some plaintive, earthy love song I'd never heard before.

I hugged myself, letting cold tendrils of rain slither down my neck.

"Jed, Jed, that's beautiful," I whispered.

He jerked his head toward me. He groaned as if suddenly sick.

"Jed, what's the—?" A sliver of cold white light appeared in the next room. We both jumped.

A woman stood in our kitchenette, half-lit by the open refrigerator. As she stooped, reaching inside, I saw a smooth downy hip, a perfect cream-colored breast topped by a dark red nipple, tiny as a chilled raspberry.

I dropped my bags and she turned on the overhead light, blinking. She stood naked, eating leftover Chinese from a carton.

She was flawlessly beautiful, an exquisite little face and wide hazel eyes. Her hair was strawberry blonde, and her skin gleamed with faint peach-colored freckles. Her waist was tiny, but her hips and breasts were lush and round. Her smile had the opaque sweetness of someone who has always been cherished. There was candid puzzlement in her eyes.

I looked to Jed. His cheeks flushed, but his jaw was set. He glared at the window.

I backed out the doorway.

I went to work. I made so much money in tips that night. I couldn't stop laughing, and all these fat businessmen and their skanky mistresses thought I was laughing at their jokes. Each time I pictured this new girl, naked and brazen in my apartment, I locked myself in the women's room and laughed until I felt like throwing up.

I'd always told Jed he taught me how to laugh. He taught me that things were never as bad as they seemed. Life in Portland was harder than we'd ever imagined; I could only get seasonal contracts with the ballet, he could barely break even with his gigs. But when we were home together, warm and laughing in that tiny amber-lit apartment, everything was okay.

When I came home from work that night, the place was deserted. The bed was rumpled, streaked with spilled honey. I lay across the green velour carpet, tapping my fingernails on the floor. My thoughts scattered like pearls from a broken string.

The sky outside lightened. A crow thumped into the window-pane. I realized with a shock that Jed and this girl were staying out on purpose—giving me plenty of time to pack.

I left just before sunrise.

Now I watch Christine emerge from the steam, her wet hair clinging to her shoulders. She's wearing a wicked little thong of white cotton. Her belly is pink.

I suck at my last cigarette, drawing up my collar against the river wind. She's everything I'm not—serene, willowy, wreathed in beauty. The air around her always seems brighter.

Jed squirms in his chair, his mouth still hanging open.

She waves an elegant, dismissive hand at him and he reluctantly returns to his music.

She rushes to the window and stands, gazing intently. I stub out my cigarette, shrinking into myself, zipping up my jacket so I'm all black leather against the black air. Does she suspect?

Ah, she's using the dark glass as a full-length mirror, as I used to.

She rubs her sides and pouts, then reaches for a bottle of lotion. Jed is still playing, but he watches her from under his curling bangs, black eyes flickering. She smoothes the lotion along her arms, her ribs, her breasts. She massages it into her thighs until the flesh glows.

Jed stands up, his teeth flashing as he tries to distract her with a joke.

She waves him down again as she runs to the closet. She's

dressing with a purpose, now, going out. Jed fits the headphones on again and gives her a defeated, watery smile as he settles into his music.

She's going out alone.

"Shit." I scramble to my feet. My boots ring over the concrete roof. Pigeons and rats go scuffling into the shadows. I descend the clanging ladder and hide behind a Dumpster.

Christine bursts through the street-level doors. She's wearing new knee-high suede boots and her fluffy blue Cookie Monster coat. She hurries down the steps, wincing and hugging herself against the chill. Even from here, I can see her tender cheeks are scarlet, her eyes tearing.

She runs to her Beamer and I fidget like a cat about to pounce. I've watched her almost every day; I've followed her to the mall, to Pilates class, to a spa. She never works, but her trips to the ATM always seem to yield a crisp stack of cash: family money. She's slumming.

My Corolla is parked at the curb; I'll be able to reach it in six steps.

Christine freezes and glances up at the apartment window, her eyes wide and stark. Something in her movement stuns me. The light falls against the perfect lines of her temple, her throat. Her skin is delicate as a child's.

I hold my breath. She seems transformed; there's something in her guilty eyes, a fault line, a crack. This might be what I've been waiting for.

She slips away from her car, walking through the alley toward the deserted riverfront. I follow more slowly, keeping close to the walls. The streetlights here are broken. Filthy mattresses lie over the sidewalks, strewn with needles and beer cans.

Christine reaches the railroad tracks and starts to run. I have to sprint to keep her bright head in my sight.

There's music near the river—a slow, hypnotic chime. It grows louder as we run. Christine turns a corner and there, beneath the freeway overpass, an old meat-processing plant is filled with energy and lemon yellow light. A giddy crowd spills over the crumbling docks. Garbage fires fill the air with acrid smoke.

Christine disappears inside. I'm breathless when I reach the door. The bouncer is hugely fat, smiling merrily. He pulls on his platinum dreadlocks as he grins at me.

"Hey, sweetheart, you old enough to be here?"

My heart is pounding. I fumble through my pockets and come up with three dollars and a bus ticket.

He laughs and grabs my wrist. He draws a black X on the back of my hand, then kisses my palm before letting me go.

The inside seems impossibly large; the plant's been gutted. I toss my jacket into a corner and the steam prickles over my bare skin. The music shakes my bones; a frantic heartbeat of a bass line under a stream of distorted, shimmering strings.

My heart is in my throat. I see Christine, half naked now, a flickering streak in the red-black heaving crowd. I approach.

I have no idea what I intend to do when I reach her. Her hair is loose, rippling around her, the opulent sun-bright hair of a Renaissance courtesan. Her skirt is short; her halter top is fastened with two ties at the back of her neck and just below her shoulders. Her waist-chain slithers over her sweaty hips. Gold bands glint on her upper arms.

I can't take my eyes off her. I've never seen her like this; there's a desperation in her movement, in her bleak, fitful glances. I feel suddenly cold. I act on instinct alone, as if this were a waking dream that would just keep unraveling as long as I kept my focus.

Sweat pools in the small of her back. She turns and smiles at a slender boy standing behind her. The invitation in her face makes me want to laugh—it's so naïve, so forlorn and pushy. They don't notice me.

Her hair whips my face. I've never been this close to her. I let my fingertips brush her ass, just tracing feather-light circles.

She turns again to the boy behind her, eyes bright. She licks her lips in a pathetic, histrionic little gesture that makes her seem whacked. He leaves. She still feels the steady touch on her ass.

I press into her before she can turn toward me. She squeals with shock.

I grab her pelvis and kiss her neck. I thought she would smell of Jed but instead there's the fragrance of gardenia soap, then the sharp, pure scent of her sweat. I push my breasts into her shoulders.

"Is this what you came here for?" I whisper, my lips resting on her ear. The music is so loud I can't hear myself. I kiss along the back of her neck, her throat, working my tongue along her jaw. I feel her moan.

She pulls my hands to her breasts. She's no longer trying to turn around and see me. I graze her neck with my teeth. She arches forward, pressing those tiny nipples into my palms.

She's so soft, so delicious, her flesh like fine sun-warmed clay under my hands.

"Stop," I hiss, still not hearing my voice over the music. "Don't draw attention to us." She drops her hands.

"Very good." I kiss her shoulder, draw my fingers along her arms. "Keep dancing, the way you were. Keep your eyes open, your face calm. No matter what I do."

Her hair is plastered to her back. I bend to kiss between her shoulder blades. She twitches but keeps swaying to the music. I rest my palms over her ass, squeezing, lifting.

Other dancers surge around us, a hot sea.

I bite her earlobe and she jumps.

"Good," I whisper, before I trace the whorls of her ear with my tongue. I reach down to her thighs and scratch her lightly with my fingernails. "Now come with me."

I turn and walk through the crowd. It's a risk; she might recognize me from behind. I move swiftly, wondering if she'll lose me completely in the darkness. But when I reach the bathroom I hear her quick, staccato breathing just behind me.

I open the door and then stand aside. She hesitates only slightly before going in. The bathroom is empty.

Panic spikes in my throat; the walls are lined with mirrors. She's sure to see me. But she's standing with her eyes closed. She keeps licking her lips. I take off my scarf and fold it, lift it over her head. The orange silk is beautiful across her eyes. I lock the door.

"You look so lovely," I tell her. She gleams in the harsh light. Her lipstick, innocent red, is streaked. Her nipples strain against the pink satin of her halter top.

"Please," she falters. She shifts her weight impatiently. Her skirt has ridden up her thighs.

"Please what?" I keep my voice gentle.

The bathroom is enormous, a factory bathroom with a half-rotted floor and a row of old urinals. One cracked window lets in the dirty fog. Every few seconds, someone pounds on the door, yelling. Let them pee outside.

Christine stumbles toward me. I back away.

"Please touch me," she whispers, ducking her head.

"Why don't you put your hands behind your back," I say kindly, biting back a laugh. "Wrists crossed."

My smile fades as she quickly complies. I'd only been half serious. Now I have to follow through.

The strange calm is still in me. I brush the back of my hand against her nipples before I move behind her. I untie her halter top and it crinkles into my palm. I caress her small wrists before I tie them together. She exhales, flexing her hands, tilting her head to the ceiling until the curling ends of her hair brush her waist.

"Why don't you take off the rest?" I lean against the sink and watch her reach to unzip her skirt. Her breasts nestle together as she moves, her hair sticks to her forehead. Finally the skirt slumps to the floor and she steps out of it, struggling to keep her balance.

She waits, smiling, wearing only her armbands, waist-chain, boots and her wisp of a thong. The drenched white cotton has darkened to silver.

"You're so pretty." I can't help saying it. I wonder for a moment if Jed has ever seen her like this. Then I can't form any more thoughts. My mouth is dry. My breasts are stinging, my palms aching for the feel of her.

She gulps, then rushes to me, pushing her white breasts against me, rolling her belly against my jeans. Her lips find my cheek, my chin.

Her desperation is almost alarming.

I grab her hair when she kisses me. She flinches but doesn't pull away. Oh, her mouth, so full of spicy, fragrant heat. It takes all my willpower not to bite her lush lower lip. I lift one leg to circle her waist and her pubic bone mashes against my clit.

I break away, panting hoarsely. "Back up," I tell her. I want to kiss her all over, free her from her boots so I can hold her small feet.

When she reaches the opposite wall, I unfasten her waist-chain, loop its ends round a cold metal pipe, then pull it tight round her hips again. She rubs her thighs together.

I fall to my knees. She jumps when she feels my breath on her belly. Her scent clouds my head, sends a searing pang to my womb. I shiver.

"Move your legs apart."

When she does I kiss her, just above the satin bow of her thong. "Very good." I take her waist-chain in my teeth and tug, playfully.

But her scent is stronger now and I'm losing control. I pull the soaked, gossamer cloth of her panties to one side. Oh, my god, she's shaved. Her mound is bare, only the faintest shadow of blonde stubble. Her labia are closed shyly, glistening like a juice-covered apricot.

"Stay still." I lean into her and brush my lips against the top of her cleft. She heaves forward and starts to grind.

She shrieks when I smack the fullest part of her ass. I look up at her. Her mouth is gaping. I rub gently where I struck.

I lift her left leg and rest her thigh on my shoulder. The suede of her boot is rough against my back. I hope she doesn't dig that heel into me.

Her labia are spread, swollen obscenely now, the inner lips unfurling toward me, raw and red. Her clit is inflamed, hard, pulsing faintly. I trace circles around it. Her cunt clenches on itself like hungry mollusk.

When I lean forward, she flinches. I smile, remembering Jed's clumsy alacrity. I lay my tongue, soft and flat, just above her clit. I look up at her and laugh, softly. I think she's holding her breath.

"Very good, Christine. I think you deserve a reward."

I don't wait for her to react at hearing her name. I close my hands around her hips and draw my tongue along her cleft, slowly and softly, more insistent with each pass. The taste of her makes me lightheaded—oysters and dark merlot. My nails dig into her ass. She'll have two neat little rows of crescent-shaped scabs.

I close my lips around her clit and nudge it with my tongue.

She shakes so violently I'm afraid she'll fall on me. Her thigh bounces on my shoulder. My tongue aches. My jaw is sore.

She nearly pulls away at the last minute but I suck her clit into my mouth, pressing my thumb against her anus. Her fingers drum against the wall, her spine stretches long and tight. I look up. Her stomach ripples. She shakes her head from side to side; her hair thrashing. Her sweat drops in my eyes, stinging me.

Finally she slumps, deathly still. I rise. My knees will ache for days.

Her mouth works soundlessly. The blindfold is damp with tears.

"So fucking lovely," I whisper. Even smeared with makeup and tears and saliva, her face is matchless. I want to lift her in my arms and take her home, to my old apartment, cover her in my finest silk sheets and brush out her glorious hair while she sleeps.

I rest my fingertips at her wet, trembling cunt. I hear my voice breaking, my words interrupted by kisses to her irresistible mouth.

"Oh, Christine, do you want more? Do you want me to keep you tied here? Do you want me to fuck you until you beg me to stop?"

She sobs once, quietly.

"Answer me, angel," I whisper into her mouth. I slide my pinky into her.

"Yes," she squeaks.

I reach around and undo the waist-chain. I free her wrists. They're only slightly marked; she didn't struggle.

"I want to see you here again soon," I say. "We can go somewhere else when you're ready. Don't you live nearby?" I watch her pulse in the hollow of her throat. We both jump when the pounding starts at the door again.

"Stay here for a bit, Christine. Don't take off your blindfold until I've gone. I'm taking your top for myself."

I lay her halter top on a sink, just in front of her.

I kiss her one last time and she rests her palms on my face. She breaks the kiss and strokes my hair. She lays her fingertips on my eyelids.

"Thank you," she murmurs. "You don't know, you don't know how much—"

I kiss her hands. Then I climb on one of the urinals and lift myself to the window.

I look down on her before I slip outside. Her face is lifted toward me, as if she could see me now through the blindfold.

The door rattles. She covers her chest and reaches for her blindfold. I jump to the alleyway below.

CRAVING MADELINE

Shanna Germain

There is nothing crueler than bringing donuts to an eating disorder group. And yet, there they sit every week, two dozen of them—the good kind, too. Cream filled, chocolate topped, with and without sprinkles, iced pink and green, they're sitting right next to the bad coffee and the nondairy creamer in little packets that have to be a hundred years old.

My group has anorexics, overeaters, bulimics, bingers— that's me—and those who are all or none of the above, almost all of them women. There's one man who comes sometimes, but he takes two donuts each time he's here, two donuts without stopping to stress, without even hesitating or caring what kind he gets, and he eats them both, in the way that normal people eat. I think he's faking it, for sympathy or women. After all, to someone with an eating disorder, donuts are never just donuts.

Maybe people think the same about me. In a group filled with bone people and fat people, and rarely in-betweens, I'm an anomaly myself, being average sized. If I work out and eat healthy most times, the binges don't wreak as much havoc on my body. I haven't binged—seriously binged—in almost six months. The group is helping, I think. Or something is.

I tend to get to the meetings late, partly because I can't stand to be in the same room with those powdery, sugary temptations for very long. But I also show up right at the last second because I like to walk in and see Madeline sitting there. She always takes the same chair—the one right across from the door. She's like a donut herself, all soft, pale curves inside a stretchy brown dress. She has this short, hot pink hair cut close to her head. I want to run my hands over it, pull her into my chest, beg her to lick the soft, sensitive curves of my breasts.

I doubt she notices me, though. I'm breakable, pale and blonde. I'm lipstick. It's the plight of the bisexual married woman to be invisible, even if the marriage is just sitting there, waiting to be ended.

I take my seat across from Madeline, where I can watch her without seeming too obvious, taking small notes of her body, her movements, the way she fills the chair as though she is comfortable with her body, with the heft and bulk of her. Madeline's got a bit of everything when it comes to eating disorders. She's the most honest—and probably the most recovered—of any of us. If I had to guess, I'd say she has willpower like nobody's business. Sitting across from her makes me feel both weak and strong. Maybe this is why she appeals to me so much; she is soft as dough and hard as the pan it's baked in.

She wears a big wooden ring on her middle finger and a million thin silver bracelets on both wrists. There's a little tattoo peeking from the inside curve of her right breast—reds and blues in a pattern I can never quite make out—but it looks like almost-clear icing on grocery store cakes.

Sometimes the group is talking about things—important

things, like how eating disorders and heart attacks go hand in hand, or how not to rot your teeth out if you're bulimic—and I realize I'm not paying attention to anything except the creamy skin of Madeline's neck and chest. Someone will say something about how her mother forced her to diet at eight, and I'll realize I've got my teeth closed tight, as though I'm closing my mouth over a fold of her skin, curling my tongue along it to pull the taste from her.

I call myself bisexual, but the truth is I've never been with a woman. And yet, I know how Madeline will taste—sugary without being cloying, refreshing as perfectly sweetened sun tea. I want to dip my head into that space between her thighs, the wet, soft place I imagine will look and feel like my own. I want to dip my fingers into her, stir her into a sweet frenzy and then taste her, suck her juice from my long fingers like the creamiest icing, the softest, most buttery frosting.

Someone shuts the door, and I lift my head with a start, realizing everyone has settled in with his or her coffee. Almost no one has a donut, though I notice Adriana, a young, pretty redhead whose fingers shake almost always from hunger, has taken a quarter of an old-fashioned (the lowest calorie of all the donuts, as I'm sure anyone in the room could tell you) and she is systematically picking it apart crumb by crumb, laying the crumbs back down on her napkin like a connect-the-dots puzzle. I tell myself I am not thinking of donuts. I tell myself I can have a donut anytime I want one, that they are not forbidden foods. This is something I've learned about binging. How counterintuitive: if I tell myself I can't have, I must have. If I tell myself I can have, whenever and however I want, I don't want. Sometimes this works.

Typically in group, we go around the circle and speak, or don't speak, depending. Our group leader is Casey, a tall, thin transsexual, a former bulimic with gorgeous skin and long, muscular legs. She developed bulimia when she was still Casey the boy, as a way to keep control, and didn't kick it until she became Casey the girl. Now, she tries to help, and I think she does a fine job, if not of helping, then of listening, which is sometimes as close to helping as someone can get.

"Well, you all know me. I'm Casey," she says, and, as always, it takes me a word or two to get used to her voice, the low tone that slightly jars coming out of her thin, lipsticked lips. "I don't see any newcomers today, so I won't talk much. I'd like to hear what you all have to say."

Casey looks to her left, where Adriana is dismantling her donut. "You want to start, please, Adriana?"

"I'm Adriana," she says without looking up. "I'm a recovering anorexic. I weigh a hundred pounds."

Liar, I think. She weighs eighty, maybe eighty-five if she wore a stone hat. And her teeth scream "throwing up," with that grayish cast that results from too much stomach acid.

This makes me sound like I've got my disorder, my life, all sewn up with a pretty little bow, doesn't it? Don't buy it. I can see my own flaws just as easily as I can see others'. Perhaps too easily. As part of our recovery, we go through our assets, are forced to see ourselves as we really are. When I focus, I can do this. I can say, "I am a little underweight, but not unhealthy. I have small, pretty breasts with big, sensitive nipples. My ass is curvy and my legs are strong. My assets are my emerald green eyes, my big smile, my long, straight hair. I am smart and funny." Sometimes I even believe it, for a little bit.

And then someone like Adriana talks about how hideous she is, how fat, how out of control. Sometimes group is harder than the disorder. If she is all of those things, what does that make me? So many, many things I don't want to be. I wish now I had grabbed a donut, two even, the ones with pink icing like Madeline's hair. I could lick it off while I listen, think of nothing but the sweet melt of sugar on my tongue and how Madeline's skin would taste in my mouth.

When Adriana is finished, Casey thanks her, then takes a moment to talk to her in a quiet voice that doesn't carry to the rest of us.

After, Casey holds her hand out to Madeline, who sits on the other side of her. Madeline's wide hand with its thick fingers wraps around Casey's long, thin fingers, the nails painted purple, the veins big and blue beneath the skin, and then Madeline smiles at Casey, and I wonder who's helping who, and if it really matters anymore.

"I'm Mad," Madeline says, like she always does. And then she flexes and growls in this way that always lightens up the group. She once said that when she stopped hiding behind food, she started hiding behind her sense of humor, that being funny was a wall to protect her from potential pain. I've never forgotten that. For weeks, I thought, *What do I have to hide behind?* and I didn't find an answer. I still haven't found an answer, but it's something, I think, to be looking at least.

"I've got a little of everything," she continues, "and I kick most of it in the ass and the balls every day with my steel-toed boots. Some days it stays down. Some days it don't. Either way, it's a little weaker when it gets up again."

She shrugs, waves a hand through the air so that her bracelets *clack-clack*. "Guess that's it."

Casey touches Madeline's shoulder. "Are you sure, honey? Because I feel like there's something else in there today."

This is what makes Casey so very good at what she does. Most people, I think, would be afraid to say that to Madeline, to this powerhouse of will and I-know-myself-ness. I would be afraid to say it to her. Hell, I'm afraid to say anything to her, and I've been coming to this group, watching her across the circle, for more than a year now.

Madeline is silent for a moment, her chin dropping to her chest with a soft inhale. And then Madeline, big strong Madeline, is crying. Not making any noise, not her, but tears are sliding off her dark mascara and running down her pale face.

"I'm." She swallows away the rest of the sentence.

Casey leans in and lifts Madeline's face in the softest movement, two fingers closing carefully over the heart-shaped point of Madeline's chin. "What, honey?" Casey asks.

"I guess I'm a little lonely," Madeline says. At the sound of those words, I feel my heart crumble apart, tiny sugar pieces that fall down through my lap. I want to crawl across the floor to kneel in the space in front of her chair, leaning my head into her thighs, asking her to stroke my head.

She smiles, a big flash of teeth and dimples, that improbably loud distress signal most people never read as anything more than pure strength, and waves away the attention focused on her. "It'll pass," she says in an almost steady voice. "You know it will."

Casey holds on a moment longer—you can see in her face she's trying to decide how hard to push, how much more to ask for—and then she nods and lets go.

"Thank you, Mad," she says. "Anyone else feeling alone? Lonely? Just a little?"

Adriana picks at her donut. Pluck. Pluck. A few other women shift and move, but no one says anything. I think about doing something stupid—raising my hand, or speaking. But I never speak at these meetings; things don't come out of my mouth very well. It's better to stay quiet. My biggest fear is that someday

Casey will call on me, that she'll see right through me and ˻
me speak, that my words will tumble and stumble in my th.˻at
until they choke me.

Casey leans back with a laugh, one of those long legs swinging
through the air, big pump hanging on by the toes. There is a
quiet teasing tone in her voice. "Well, since everyone else's life
is perfect and not lonely at all—I know mine sure is—let's talk
about the other things that are perfect with our lives, shall we?
Who wants to start?"

The next week there are no donuts. There is no Madeline either,
and I sit in my chair, staring at the empty space across from
me. I have a brief moment where I wonder if it's Madeline who
actually brings the donuts, if she's the one who has such a cruel
heart. But somehow, I don't allow myself to believe it.

Either way, I'm glad there are no donuts here. Usually, being
in front of people is enough in itself to keep me from binging,
but today, with the dull beat inside my chest at the sight of
Madeline's empty chair, I'm not so sure. I have coffee in a cup,
and I break the Styrofoam bits off the rim, *crack-crack*.

All week long, every time I wanted to eat, I thought of Madeline, of Madeline saying she was lonely, of those silent tears. I'd
close my eyes and pretend her big, curvy body was pressing hard
to mine, her hands tracing the curves of my lips. I'd suck her
fingers into my mouth, way back deep in my throat, groaning
around them as her other hand fumbled with my jeans. I wanted
to eat nothing but her body, nipples melting like nonpareils
along my tongue, to crack open her legs and chew the soft fat
at the inside of her thighs, to suck the tight pink flesh of her clit
into my mouth like a tiny oyster.

Casey clears her throat and starts the session by talking
about addiction and compulsion: what it means and how we

cope. She doesn't say anything about the missing Madeline.

"Caroline? You want to say something this week?"

I swallow back my hot coffee, letting it scald my tongue, and shake my head. I don't know what I'd say even if I could say something. I want chips and cookies. I want to stuff and stuff myself until I can't breathe or think or want.

"You sure?" Casey asks.

I nod, my eyes closing to shut out her voice and the way it doesn't mix with the rest of her; to shut out pretty, tiny Adriana and her chipped blue nail polish; to shut out the empty chair across the circle from me.

My fingers are shaking as they pick at the cup rim and there is the thing I don't want to admit—that perhaps it isn't the group, or Casey's quiet voice that's been helping me. Maybe it's just that I've traded one addiction for another, craving fats and sugars exchanged for craving Madeline.

I almost don't go the next week. All week long I've eyed candy in bags, the kind that can be eaten one after another without thinking, cookies as big as a plate, thick slabs of cheddar cheese that could be torn into hunks and eaten with my fingers. I won't. I won't. But I wonder, what if I show up and there is no Madeline? What will I eat? The answer scares me.

Instead, I show up early, too early. No one's there yet. The coffee hasn't even been made. But there are donuts. And there is Madeline, setting them on the table at the back of the room.

"O-Oh," I say. The air stutters out of my mouth, makes a sound.

She turns to look at me, bracelets clacking quietly. "Casey asks me to bring them. Says it helps her get a handle on where everyone's at by how they eat or don't eat the donuts."

She lifts her shoulders. "Think it's some kind of test for me, too. But I've been doing it for a year now. Hardly bothers me anymore."

I can only stand there, stupidly, wishing I had something in my throat to make words with. Finally, I do the only thing I can—I move my body forward and I touch her wrist, the place where all her bracelets bend and clack together.

She catches her breath, quiet, not breathing at all, making the place where her tattoo rests go still. I bend my head forward, lick her blue-and-red skin like it's the finest icing, and her exhale is warm against my ear. She makes my tongue taste like sweet salt, like caramel corn and coffee, and I swallow her flavor down, a quiet groan going with it, all the way to my stomach, all the way to the soft melt between my thighs.

Madeline's hand is in my hair, *clack-clack* of bracelets, and she's holding me against her. I breathe her in, trace the outline of her design with my tongue. She tastes as good as I expected. Better. I want to eat her up. Oysters on the half shell to be sucked down, salted caramel to be licked into melting, the crunch of candy between my teeth. She is the flavor of everything I've ever wanted to stuff myself with but didn't, sweet and sour, salvation and sustenance.

"Y-you don't ha-have to be a-alone," I say. I want to say more—I always want to say more—but words are so hard for me. The way I choke around them, crumbs that tickle my throat and make me cough each one into the air.

"Oh, honey," Madeline says. "I'm no cure for you. I'm no cure for anybody."

"I d-don't," I say, and the saying of it exhausts me. It's all I have, these broken words. They're not enough. They're never enough.

I pull back, trying to swallow all the words so I can breathe again, but Madeline tightens her hands in my hair. She leans my head back so that I am looking up at her, and then she touches my mouth to hers. Soft, plummy lips mash against mine, her mouth sucking my tongue in until it no longer belongs to me, until she is eating me up and I want nothing more than the sound she is making right now, this hungry slurp as she swallows me whole.

CALL ME CLEOPATRA

Gabrielle Foster

It was autumn. I remember that, the smell, as if the desert were smoldering, creosote going to ash, the electricity in the air as the city filled up with students. I remember I was drawing—I do not remember what exactly, although I could probably go back and find the exact page in my sketchbook, that ink sketch of a passerby or fire hydrant. I might even be able to discern the moment, the fraction of a second when my pen skipped, a wobble in a previously straight line, when she asked to bum a smoke.

She was dressed like the street kids sprawled on the city sidewalks, haute vagabond, in a pale saffron dress embroidered with fraying fleur-de-lis. Her skin was tanned bronze, her hair titian. She had a tangle of necklaces at her throat and wide bands of leather on each wrist.

I slipped a cigarette from my pack and handed it to her. She reached across the table and snatched my lighter, jamming her other hand into the deep pocket of her dress and rocking back on her heels. The lighter snapped, the cigarette flared, and she exhaled a plume of blue smoke. She cocked her head to the side. "Thanks," she said. "I'll see you again."

I looked for her in the coffee shop after that, glancing furtively at the door, scanning the other tables. When I caught myself looking up each time the door opened, I pinched the inside of my wrist and picked up my pen. Days passed before I heard the voice again.

"You have such a graceful neck."

I looked up from my sketchbook. The woman was standing over me with a gleam in her eyes. Her red hair was tousled beneath a crushed velvet beret and she wore a black shirt of raw silk. She was wearing the same collection of necklaces and bracelets as before. She gestured at the empty seat across from me. I nodded.

She slipped into the seat before I could say anything and began pulling items out of a tapestry purse: tubes of lipstick, a fringed scarf, loose change, a dog-eared address book. I watched her as if she were spreading out Tarot cards before telling my fortune. The woman found what she was looking for, a slim pack of cigarettes.

She squinted at me through the smoke, her jade eyes thickly lined with kohl. "Have you ever noticed how strangers will always say the same thing to you? It's always *beautiful eyes, what a lovely smile.*"

She looked at me, arching one eyebrow, and tapped her cigarette against the rim of the ashtray between us. "I'd guess people tell you you've got beautiful eyes," the woman said. "You're not the type to smile often. But your neck is a swan's, a dancer's. Every time someone tells me I have a beautiful smile, I say *all the better to eat you with!*" She reached around her neck and undid a clasp. She held out a slim band of midnight blue velvet. "I've been keeping this for you," she said. "It matches your eyes."

I stammered something, waving the necklace away in protest. The stranger pushed the necklace across the table toward me, where it lay coiled between us like a viper. She jutted her chin at my sketchbook. "You an artist?"

I mumbled something. "Well, I draw."

"What do you draw?"

"Plants. Flowers."

"Looks to me like you draw ashtrays." She winked.

"Sometimes I just draw whatever's in front of me."

The redhead stuck out her leg, turning it to the left and to the right, scrutinizing it, and hitched her black stockings up from the ankle. She rested her chin in her hand and considered me. My shoulders tensed; I waited for the inevitable questions, bent bobby pins working to pick a lock. "Do you draw people?" she asked. "Would you like to draw me?"

I lit a cigarette, fumbling with my lighter. I could see the woman sitting still as my hands moved over my sketchbook, capturing the planes of her face. I thought briefly of the old belief that images steal the soul. Could I steal a piece of someone's soul with a portrait?

"I'm not very good," I protested.

"You seem all right at ashtrays. How much worse could it be?"

Her name was Cricket, and the neighborhood she lived in must have been fashionable once, but the large houses were now subdivided, the yards overgrown. Shutters hung from their hinges, porches sagged; the street smelled of grease, aerosol, onions.

We climbed two flights of stairs to reach her apartment. It was almost bare, one long room flanked by chipped columns. French doors led out to a narrow balcony; the doors were open, their long white curtains billowing in the breeze. The room smelled faintly of cat urine. The walls were covered in peeling wallpaper, a muted assemblage of tea roses. Sycamores shaded the few windows and the room was gloomy with shadows.

At one end of the large room there was a futon bed, dressed in rumpled black sheets, beneath a narrow window bordered in stained glass squares. At the other end a writing desk was pushed against the wall. There was no other furniture. Suitcases and carpetbags were piled in a far corner; clothes spilled haphazardly across the floor, a sprawl of colors and textures. A large black cat with an opaque eye hunched on a pile of clothes, hissing when I passed.

There were shelves of brick and board at the head of the bed, weighed down with a stereo, paperbacks, stacks of CDs. Strewn with votives and tapered candles, the shelves gave the impression of an altar. Statuettes of the Virgin Mary struck various pious poses, looking heavenward or at their feet, hands clasped. Rosary beads and dried flowers hung from thumbtacks and the necks of the figures.

I asked her if she was Catholic, my voice too loud in the cavernous room. I glanced across the heavy shelves, at the tarnished silver crosses lying in dust and fragments of dried petals.

Cricket sat down on the bed beside me and lifted one of the Marys. "My mother's mother was a nun and my father's mother was burnt at the stake as a witch," she said. "Have you ever been burnt at the stake? It's an awful way to go. If the executioner likes you he piles more wood on the fire so you burn faster; if he doesn't he lets you roast slowly for hours."

Cricket smiled and ran her thumb across the Virgin's placid face. "Me, I don't believe in God, or God doesn't believe in me. Either way it amounts to the same. You want to split a veggie pita?"

Cricket stared into the wan light of the fridge. It was as empty as the room. She grabbed two bottles of beer from the vegetable crisper and a take-out bag and walked back to the futon. She spread the fast-food wrapper out on the sheet and handed me a beer. I took a sip. It was dark, bitter.

Cricket asked, "Do you like Billie Holiday?" She rolled onto her stomach, fiddling with the stereo.

It was a hot day and a few of the windows were open. A sweet-smelling breeze drifted in, unfurling its willow green scent.

Cricket reclined, propped up on her elbow, and lit a cigarette with her free hand. The crescent of her breast was visible beneath the open neck of her shirt. I studied her, the beret, the silk, the kohl, the mass of bracelets at each wrist. I wondered what Cricket's shirt would feel like if I rubbed the collar between my fingers. The fabric looked so thick and would be warm from her skin.

Cricket smoked her cigarette and I took long swallows of the beer, trying to finish it. The pita sandwich sat untouched on its wrapper between us. The cool breeze was distracting; it tickled at my skin and reeked of promise. "You don't sound like a Texan," Cricket said. "Where are you from?"

I told her about Boston and my father's manicured lawn, the cobblestone streets and wrought iron lampposts. I talked about the college of stone and ivy and my mother the magician who made herself disappear. I talked about coming to the desert and the horizon that goes on for miles.

"What about you," I said. "Where are you from?"

Cricket laughed and wrinkled her nose. "I'm from the meadow and the ice plains and the cities where the buildings are stacked on each other like books," she said. "I was washed up on the riverbed in a crib made of birch bark. I rose up like a flame from my father's cracked skull. I have no mother and no father."

"Who are you, really?"

"Who am I? I'm a woman made of clouds. I'm only a dream. We're all only dreams."

"Cricket. That's an unusual name."

"Call me Cleopatra," she said. "Call me Helen of Troy. I will call you Delilah, Andromeda, Proserpina. I will call you button and plum."

The first time we had dinner together I wore a black cotton dress, the only dress I had brought with me to Texas. The moment Cricket opened the door, I knew the dress was a mistake. Hers was dark jade and the color made her eyes glow. Her hair was sleekly coiffed, a few tendrils framing her face. An emerald pendant hung at her throat from a silver strand. The assemblage of bracelets had been exchanged for wide twin bands of hammered silver.

And me in my black baggy dress, like an insect with a dark carapace: a dung beetle, a cockroach.

She had a bottle of beer in one hand and a cigarette in the other. When she kicked the door shut behind me, she told me I looked smashing.

I could not return the compliment. I wasn't going to fall for that. I bit my lip. We were off to a bad start, starting off with charity. I glanced around for a spot to sit and settled on the futon as I had before, brushing a drift of loose dollar bills from the sheets. I folded and unfolded my hands in my lap, leaned forward and backward, crossing and uncrossing my legs. I had underestimated the trouble of limbs and appendages, their limitless capacity for awkwardness.

Cricket did not sit, she did not pause, she was a dragonfly darting between cattails. She popped the top off a beer and handed it to me. She gathered bits of things and tucked them into her purse, checked her hair in the mirror, swept clutter from the kitchen counter into a drawer. She chattered and I offered murmurs and mumbled responses. I had fallen into a chasm in the ground, I was falling and falling, the light going dim above me.

Cricket fussed with hairpins, loose change, keys. She was chattering about the restaurant she was going to take me to, but I did not hear her. I worried about the dress. I saw a stain I hadn't noticed earlier, a smudge on my lap; ink, most likely, wiped from my hands while I was distracted, drawing. The dress was sleeveless and I could not remember if I had shaved under my arms or if the deodorant I was wearing was the type that left residue like chalk dust on the skin. Would I have to spend the evening with my arms pinned to my sides? My heart hammered, my face felt flushed, there was a roaring in my head like the surf. Cricket was fiddling with her necklace in the mirror; she turned away for just a moment, and I glanced at the beer she had given me. The beads of perspiration on the brown glass stood out in sharp focus. I tilted the bottle and an amber juice sloshed across my lap.

There was perfect silence as I leapt to my feet.

"Your dress," she cried. I held my breath. Then, mercifully, she began to laugh. The riot of her laughter dissolved my rib cage into a shower of stars and in that moment we were friends, conspirators, children.

"You can't go out like that," she said. "I'll lend you something of mine." She crouched in the corner of the room over piles of vinyl, satin, velvet, sifting through them as if she were about to deliver an incantation.

The shower curtain was mildewed, the toilet and sink mazy with dark cracks. Cricket walked in, shaking out a baby blue dress. There was a design etched into the fabric: palm fronds, tropical.

"You're wearing my choker," she said. She ran her finger approvingly over the band at my throat. I had put it on at the last minute, darting back in just as I was about to lock up, snatching it from the top of the dresser.

When she left, I lifted the black dress over my head and draped it over the metal shower rod, where it hung like a reproach. I was not, by nature, deceptive; this was my first ruse. A ruse, I thought. It made me feel clever. I considered the blue dress, holding it out with outstretched arms, debating whether to step into it or slip it over my head. I remember inching it over my hips, sucking in my stomach, holding my breath. Had I any belief in God, I would have prayed fervently not to hear the sound of the delicate fabric tearing. I managed to zip it up most of the way and smiled at my reflection in the mirror. I tried to arch one eyebrow, the way Cricket had in the coffee shop, but I did not know which muscles to move.

When I stepped out of the bathroom, Cricket moved to inspect me. She zipped the dress the rest of the way, swift as my mother had been at zipping me into winter coats when I was a child. "We should do something about your hair," she said, talking more to herself than me. She pushed aside vials and bottles on the writing desk, picking out barrettes and a handful of bobby pins. I stood very still as she did my hair in that same brisk manner. Up close, she smelled like sweet cream. I could feel her breath warming my neck. I ran my hands over my bare arms when she stepped away.

"We'll do something better with it later," she said, smoothing down a lock of my hair. "You would look lovely with gold high-lights."

My shoulders sagged. I was Galatea: possibly lovely, if only someone would chip away the rest of this coarse stone.

* * *

What a night that was, that first night, how dizzying and horrifying and wonderful. I had never seen anyone make an entrance as Cricket did, sweeping into the restaurant, announcing our presence. I smiled at the maitre d', hoping to catch his eye: *There are two of us here,* I wanted to say, stabbing my finger at his little book. *Reservations for two.* But he did not look at me as he led us to our table. As we moved through the restaurant, the diners paused, frozen, forks halfway to their mouths, as Cricket glided past them. She ordered wine for both of us, and I fussed overly long with my linen napkin, unfolding it in my lap and arranging it. What would I have to do, I wondered, to make someone notice me? Upset the table? Throw food? Set the draperies on fire?

Cricket leaned across the table. "You look great," she whispered. "No one can take their eyes off of you." Her smile was inclusive; I was grateful for it. Despite the warmth of the restaurant, I felt chilled, and I could not bring myself to look directly at her. My jaw felt pinned shut; I fidgeted with the silverware, moving everything over an inch, lining up the forks and knives and spoons so that their stems were even. I sipped at my ice water and discreetly, beneath the cover of the tablecloth, dug my thumbnail into the pad of my palm over and over again, leaving a red welt.

Cricket masked over my silence. She talked about the clothing shops in Austin, the ones she shopped at, which ones were overpriced, which ones had the tackiest, the cheapest, the trendiest merchandise. She dropped shop names like passwords into a secret world: *Togs A-go-go, Glad Rags. The Good Foot,* where you could find fabulous platform shoes and thigh-high leather boots in every color. She said *fabulous* a lot. This particular mail-order catalogue, *Hellabore,* was the best, the most outra-

geous. She had ordered a vinyl vest last month, lilac, zippered
up the front and cut down to here, and they carried hosiery with
seams. And as for music, she continued, well, you were in luck in
Austin. You could walk into any of the little nightclubs squeezed
together on Sixth Street and hear fabulous music: jazz, blues,
swing, zydeco, hard rock, soft rock, reggae, ska—and what did
I listen to? Oh, well, you could find that anywhere. The dance
clubs, though—that's where the real action was, house music,
hip-hop, synth-pop, trip-hop, acid-house, techno, rave. We'd
drop by her favorite spot after dinner. I was game, yes?

Cricket stabbed the air with her fork, slashed with the side of
her hand, and made sweeping gestures as she spoke. I felt I should
be taking notes, scribbling these names on a crib sheet, where
Cricket shopped, where she went at night. But I couldn't keep up
with her; I was mesmerized by the birdlike motions of her hands,
the exotic notes spilling from her lips like smooth stones, *hip-
hop, trip-hop*. Perhaps beauty was contagious. Perhaps beautiful
people were like phagocytes, those engulfing, cleansing cells, their
luminous membranes reaching out to encompass their compan-
ions. I imagined myself being swallowed up in an epithelial layer,
the mucilaginous film covering my eyes and transforming me,
rendering me into a creature radiant and sublime.

"But who are you," I asked her.

She laughed. "I'm a beekeeper," she said. "I'm an astronaut.
I'm the queen of a country that hides under the sea. Who are
you?"

We went to parties under city bridges, in abandoned facto-
ries, dance clubs. Each morning as dawn broke we crashed into
her room, knocking over empty wine bottles by the door. We
collapsed onto the futon like daredevil divers, attempting a
landing in a small pool of water from a great height.

Cricket had shoes with impossible straps, a dozen slim bands snaking up her ankle, wide buckles, intricate knots. Some nights she would lean over to undo them and not be able to complete the task. She would fall back, laughing. "I can't do it," she gasped. "Please, get them off me."

"Why do you wear these things," I laughed. The attempt to tease was a risk; I was made bold by gin and wine. I lifted myself from the futon, bending over Cricket's feet.

"Beauty...suffering," Cricket sighed. "Like the Queen in 'Snow White,' the fairy tale, not the movie, forced to dance in white-hot iron shoes. That's me. Oh, everything is spinning."

"You might at least have one pair of sensible shoes, for dancing."

"God as my witness, I will never wear sensible shoes." Cricket laughed and laughed.

"You're so difficult." I remember my slight smile, then, indulgent. Finally the straps loosened and the shoe gave.

Cricket reclined languorously, stretching her arms over her. The soft skin on the inside of her arms was dotted with tiny red bumps. Mosquitoes loved her, she had said, her blood was so sweet. Her wrists were wrapped in dark leather cuffs.

"Difficult? Am I really?" She sighed. "I'm beautiful, though; that makes up for it. Tell me I'm beautiful."

I laughed and turned away. My laugh sounded easy, a match for hers in the shadowy room. The other shoe was less tightly bound, and it slipped off Cricket's foot as she rolled over onto her stomach. Her mascara was smudged, her eyes smoky in the moonlight. She had been chain-smoking and laughing loudly all night, and her voice had grown husky. I lay back on the bed, slowly. The room rippled around me, the walls buckling, the ceiling fluid.

* * *

I was not used to drinking then. The music at the parties was earth, the solid ground holding everything together, and the people swaying and maneuvering through the room were a harvest of flowers. Faces swam into my field of vision—corollas of beige, fawn, mahogany—and then out again. Cricket was always surrounded, men lighting her cigarettes, women laughing at her stories, never quite taking their eyes off her. I watched them watch her; I discerned, in that slight narrowing of their eyes, their distrust of her. They cast the same uncertain gaze on me, for my nearness to her. Their caution thrilled.

"I've never known anyone with so many friends," I told her one night as we lay sprawled on the black sheets of the futon.

I tried to interpret her smile. I was an anthropologist who had not yet spent enough time with the natives to understand their nuances of expression, their inflections. Her laughter rumbled up from the soles of her feet. "Friends," she scoffed. "What friends? I have no friends. Does a beekeeper count the bees as friends? An astronaut the stars?"

Cricket extinguished her cigarette and there was silence for a long time, until I was sure she had fallen asleep. She lay still as if she were carved of stone. I wished I had my sketchpad. Her eyelashes were dark and thick; I could imagine rendering them with one sweep of charcoal. She lay awry in her sleep, hips and shoulders at perpendicular angles. I knew exactly how I would shape the geometry of her body, the triangles meeting together, how I would begin to sketch the smooth curves of her arms, the jutting ridge of scapula. The right blade of her hip was cocked like a bowl turned on edge, but I could not see the position of her legs, obscured as they were by the dim light. The right leg must be bent, crossing over the other; her knee resting on the mattress. To be certain, I reached out, hesitating only a moment, and grazed my hand over her hip, feeling for the intersection where the shelf of her pelvis bisected into her legs.

She shifted in her sleep and I jerked my hand away. When she murmured something I closed my eyes and feigned sleep.

She rolled over, her hand brushing my waist. I could smell the wine on her breath. "Have you fallen in love with me yet?" Her voice was thick with sleep.

"Are you dreaming?"

She turned her back to me. "You want to leave," she said.

"Do you want me to leave?"

She took my hand in hers and pressed my fingertips to her lips. Her lips were cool on my fingertips, on the cup of my palm. The moonlight through the windowpanes cast diamonds on my legs. I asked her, "What am I to you?"

"You are a dream I would like to dream," she said. "It's better to dream than have a lover. When you wake up from a dream you can tell yourself it wasn't real at all."

Her lips pressed against my lips, my neck. I had never felt anything like her softness. It was a field of poppies, their velvety throats opening to the sun. When I moved my hands I could not interpret my own gestures. The arc of my wrist as I rested my hand against her breast was either a brace connecting us or a shield.

SKINNY-DIPPING

Angela Caperton

When Maxine vaulted onto the sagging mattress, she almost tossed Regina off the bed.

"Enough, Gina," Maxine growled as she clamped on to Regina's heavy book and threw it halfway across the room.

"Hey, Max, a little respect, please," Regina pleaded. "Even used, that book cost me eighty bucks."

"Crack that book again today, Gina and I'll burn it." Maxine pulled out her lighter and flicked.

"Fine," Regina snapped as she retrieved the book and tossed the *Norton Anthology of European Literature* onto the bed. So much for Dante. She shoved at the thick ropes of her red hair until they fell down her back. Hands on her hips, she faced off with Maxine. "Will you explain to my father why I failed lit?"

Maxine, with her rich espresso skin and long-lashed, almost black eyes, reminded Regina of the painting that had brought her to Shelby University and their exalted art history program. She'd been a junior in high school when she'd traveled to Huntington to see one of the rare exhibits that departed from antebellum nostalgia. The image on the canvas had taken her breath away. The Queen of Sheba, splayed upon a sea of pillows, arching against an unknown passion, arms stretching over her head in surrender and triumph. The painting vibrated with sexuality and Regina stood frozen, staring, then blushing as an ache and an unexpected dampness settled between her legs. It had been the first nude oil painting Regina had ever seen in person. In that instant she fell in love with art—and to some extent, with Sheba.

Looking at her roommate, Regina wondered again if God had a twisted sense of humor. Maxine looked fresh and vital, her short, sassy hair angled perfectly with her jawline. She flashed a smile—a shy curve of painted bronze that held a shimmer of mischief. "Sure, Gina. Then I'll tell him all about you fucking Professor Sanchez in his office."

Regina's cheeks burned. "Professor Sanchez isn't teaching this course."

Maxine grinned. "No wonder you're failing." Her smile turned to laughter. "You should think about it. Professor Emmel isn't bad looking for an old white woman, and honey," Maxine winked, wicked delight radiating, "oysters are a delicacy." She kissed Regina lightly on her cheek then practically danced toward her dresser.

"Look," Maxine announced as she stripped off her tight blue jeans. "Les and I are meeting some friends at the quarry." She skinned out of her T-shirt, freeing perfect little breasts with purple nipples, and Regina ached at the sinuous beauty, the dimples of Maxine's spine; the round, tight orbs of her ass; long, defined thighs and all that beautiful, dark skin.

Maxine rattled open one of the dresser drawers and removed a skimpy, hot pink bikini.

She looked over her shoulder at Regina, one ebony eyebrow

arched. Her lips pressed together into a stern line then she sucked
in a chastising *tsk* as she pulled the strings of the halter around
her neck. "Girl, you've got about ten minutes to get dressed."

"Dressed?" Regina looked down at her red sweatpants and
T-shirt.

"I told you. We're going to the quarry. You'll roast in that
outfit."

"I'm not going. I have a paper due Monday. So do you."

Maxine turned around, hands on her hips, clenching the
skimpy fuchsia bottoms. Regina locked her gaze on Maxine's,
even as the teasing shadow between Maxine's legs dared Regina
to stare. "Gina, I promised my gramma I wouldn't commit
assault this semester. Don't make me crack a chair over your
head and break her heart. Get dressed."

Regina dug her painted toes into warm sand, the brim of her
Panama hat shielding her face from the blazing sun. Laughter,
music, the exotic scent of sunning oils, and the diamond splash
of water turned the day golden. Regina watched Maxine and
Les, Maxine's black hair glittering with droplets and Les's arms
around her supporting her weight as he spun with her until they
fell into the water, laughing. They kissed long and deep, bodies
moving, hands stroking, promising, and Regina knew what she
wanted for herself: a kiss from a lover.

Movement caught her gaze. Regina looked over at a bouncing
blonde, a beer in one hand, her barely covered tits jiggling over a
stomach too flat to have seen food in the last month.

Carmen began to dance with Allen Greenwall, shaking her
ass against his crotch, sliding along his body as she might a
shining silver pole.

Regina wrinkled her nose.

Not Carmen.

Maxine.

She fell back against the sandy bank, pulled the Panama over her eyes, and tried to make sense of her whirling emotions. What was wrong with her?

She watched the other young men and women splashing in the quarry water, the casual flirtation and the occasional couple locked in slippery embrace. A boy like Les, she thought, like David back home. They slept together the night of the senior prom and sex with him felt good, but not magical, like she hoped it would. Since then, there really hadn't been anyone.

She watched a boy scramble up one of the sandy, manmade hills around the quarry pit. Almost naked, lean and muscled, he scaled the steep incline like a monkey.

With a delighted, exuberant yawp, he launched himself, arms spread wide, back arched, no grace, no style, all play.

His flat impact raised a geyser of spray. The collective cringe of the crowd broke into male bluster and laughter as others scrambled to outdo him. A chorus of female warnings cheered the guys as they raced up the loose sand.

Sometimes, Regina thought, *that's what it takes. A leap.*

The whole mood of the quarry changed, as though the boy's daring flight had been a signal that anything might be possible. The swimming and splashing in the pit turned wilder. Someone started a game of horse, and girls mounted on their boyfriends' shoulders pushed and pulled at one another. Regina wanted to be out there among them, but she remained planted on the bank, outside and a little lonely.

Carmen squealed as another girl claimed her top, the blonde's big breasts bouncing out of control. Someone whooped and raucous shrieks rang in the rocky bowl of the quarry. Cheers became hoots as another girl stripped, then a guy on the shore, not ten feet from Regina, kicked his trunks away, his cock not hard, but not soft either, and ran back into the water. Bathing suits and surfer trunks sailed out of the quarry to land in wet bundles on the shore, as Regina realized she might be the only person in the vicinity who wasn't naked.

She saw Maxine, her bikini top gone, probably her bottoms too, beads of water dripping from her nipples as Les held her from behind, his arms possessively around her middle, his chest pressed tight against her back.

Moving.

Moving.

Maxine's black hair was smoothed back, her thick lashes against her cheek. Gina watched her roommate's arm encircle Les's neck as she arched, her mouth opening then closing, her teeth catching her lower lip, Les's hand cupping one dark nipple, rubbing, taunting, teasing. The way he held her, he might be...

Regina cupped her crotch and squeezed her legs together, wanting to leave, wanting to stay, needing, needing more.

Moving.

Moving.

Until the hill swallowed the sun in a blazing outline of molten gold and brought the day and the play to their inevitable ends, hiding what happened out in the water, except from Regina's imagination.

Maxine took her shopping for a bathing suit the next day. Regina chose a tankini of dark, shining olive and a matching sarong. She looked good in the scraps of green material. Her legs were long and showed more shape than she expected, not long like Maxine's and not nearly so defined, but nice. She hadn't purposely tried to lose any weight when she came to Shelby, but between Maxine's dancer's diet, walking miles every day on campus and the absence of anything tasty for miles, she had soon found her pants falling off her hips. Regina's button-down shirts no longer puckered open at her breasts. She wasn't skinny, she never would be, nor did she care if she was or wasn't. She never knew a time when she wasn't at least well fleshed but in the months at Shelby, it wasn't just the toning of her legs or the inches dropped from her waist. She seemed rounder, softer than before. Now, in the dressing room, when she looked at her breasts cupped by the olive green material, her smile widened. They were full mounds, their shape perfect, nipples hard buttons pushing against the silky material. She wondered what the top would look like when it was wet.

It was Tuesday. The following week her world would revolve around midterm prep and a paper on the Pre-Raphaelite Brotherhood. Hundreds of pages of research and study awaited her, but as the days melded into endless study, her thoughts returned again and again to the sunlight diamonds on the quarry waters, the riot of skin and play that she had been at the edge of, like a fantasy of someone else's life, like a vision of her own desire.

The next Saturday, Regina spread a wide towel the color of neon raspberry on the narrow shore, put her straw bag down and turned to look at the people splashing and playing in the water.

"Looking for someone?" Maxine bumped Regina's hip with her own and grinned.

"No," Regina replied, surprised by her own truthfulness. "Just looking."

Maxine stroked her arm. "Come on, Gina. No excuses this time." Warm, like the brush of pillowed silk upon her skin, Maxine kissed her cheek and whispered, "Don't make me and Les toss you in."

As Maxine walked into the water, Gina saw her as a painting, a primal Venus, dark and glorious, returning to the sea, bold strokes of rich tones, umbers and reds, the water a mirror of a sky streaked with the brilliant oranges of dusk. And Maxine, the bikini gone in Regina's imagination, was a vision with her thick mane curving over her dark skin teasing purple nipples taut with lust, her lithe, tight body beaded with water and sweat, her gaze drawing men and women to the sea, to her arms, and love divine.

"Gina!"

"What?" she replied too loudly, her heart tripping over her reverie.

"Two seconds."

"I'm coming, I'm coming," Gina grumbled as she shed her sarong and followed Maxine into the water. The heat of the afternoon sun caressed her shoulders with a lover's stroke. The water cuffed her ankles and the sand massaged her feet as she walked into the pit's edge. The lukewarm surface hid chilled silk as the silted floor fell away. It had been years since Regina had swum, but a familiar exuberance sang inside her. She filled her lungs and dove, immersing herself. Light wrapped her in gossamer ribbons.

Regina rose to the surface beside Maxine and grinned.

"See, Gina? Sometimes you just need to take a chance."

Regina watched the beads wink and dance on Maxine's skin, and her mouth became the desert. Maybe Maxine was right.

Maybe.

Regina settled her feet upon the bottom, the water reaching her neck, but she stepped up to her roommate, giddy with the pounding of her own heart, fear and wonder and want tangling together in her stomach and brain until all Regina saw were the drops of moisture on Maxine's shoulders, and only the exotic tickle of Maxine's scent filled her nose.

Regina wanted her roommate's lips. She wanted to taste

every part of Maxine's lush mouth, but not yet. No, when she finally kissed Maxine, Regina wanted that moment to be more than fearful fumbles and sloppy smacks.

She stroked up Maxine's arm under the surface, the water adding an erotic gloss to the dark girl's skin. Silky juice ran like a current in Regina's blood, under her green trunk, flesh slick and sensitive with want.

Maxine faced Regina, her smile full and true, her gaze amused, then intrigued as Regina pressed closer.

Regina's heart raced like an engine as she closed her eyes and pressed her lips to Maxine's shoulder, drinking in precious jewels as the back of her fingers deliberately caressed the perfect orb of Maxine's Lycra-covered breast.

She pulled away and smiled, tickled by Maxine's almost stunned expression.

Sunlight bloomed in her own smile. "You're right, Maxine. Sometimes, you just have to take a chance and leap...."

Buoyant, Regina moved away, backstroking to shore. Rockets soared in her veins and the ache in her sex stole her breath. Time held the key now. Her brother, a sous-chef in Mobile, had taught her much about the value of patience.

Fine wine aged, and fantastic feasts required hours, sometimes days of preparation.

Maxine had put the pot on the stove; all Regina had done was turn on the heat.

In the days after, things were different between her and Maxine. A layer of formality had been shed. Regina couldn't read Maxine's thoughts or feelings. Maybe she wasn't supposed to. Life was a journey, and sometimes the fun came when there were no maps.

The roommates bore down for the last week of the semester.

Life blurred into an endless wade through texts and Internet research with the occasional surfacing for food. By Thursday, the brutal finals week seemed interminable.

Regina didn't remember returning to the dorm after her last exam in her political science class. Like a zombie, she stumbled into her room and fell on her bed. Just after noon on Friday, her bladder and Maxine's stereo pouring out Rihanna coaxed Regina back from the dead.

"There you are, girl. I was about to call the paramedics. Feel like a swim?"

Regina rose and moved to where Maxine leaned against the bathroom doorframe, the smile on her face impish.

"Isn't Les's anatomy final today?"

Maxine shoulders rose in a nonchalant shrug. "Yes, at three." She stood near Regina, the tiny bathroom suddenly very warm. "I'm a big girl, Gina. I don't need a lifeguard."

Regina reached for her toothbrush, eager for something to curl her fingers around. "Yes, I'd like a swim."

Maxine grinned at her through the reflection in the small mirror over the sink. Like a wisp, she slid away, giving Regina a playful slap on the ass. "Good. Get dressed then. I'll get the cooler."

Regina wet her brush and didn't exhale until she heard the door shut.

At the quarry, the sun turned the sandy bank to glittering sugar and heated the Panama on Regina's head. She stared at the sparse crowd celebrating in the warm water of the pit. Maybe twenty people dotted the shorelines, but by sunset, fires, beer, and exuberance would cram every available space. She laid out her blanket, claiming her place, then followed Maxine's lead and removed her sarong from around her hips.

Maxine rolled onto her stomach. One slender, bare foot lay

warm against Regina's calf, sending a shiver up her spine with the soft insistence of Maxine's toe trailing along the muscle to her ankle. Something passed between them, intangible but as real as the sun in the sky. Maxine sat up and looked at her, dark eyes depthless and bright with mischief. She nodded her head toward the water and Regina smiled and sat up.

Grinning, Maxine reached behind her back and untied her pink bikini top. Her perfect creamy coffee breasts filled Regina's vision. Maxine stood up, dragging Regina's gaze up with her, and silently challenged her. She answered the call, removing her tankini top and tossing it atop the neon scrap of Maxine's stringed halter.

Maxine laughed and stepped to the quarry's edge, slipping into the water. The breeze stiffened Regina's nipples as the sun kissed her pale skin to instant warmth. She looked around the quarry and wondered how many of the people there were watching her, how many of them could see that she had crossed a border and would never look back.

She tossed her hat on the bank then slid into the water, following Maxine, light with freedom from class work and expectations, floating on the knowledge that she was one step closer to her goals. She swam with long strokes to Maxine's side, then stood on the silted bottom and looked at her roommate, arms easily sculling the water, limbs like mystical, half-hidden wings.

They swam together with lazy strokes until the water concealed them from their ribs down, the bank of the quarry twenty feet away. No other swimmers splashed nearby. The dull weight between Regina's thighs began a slow pulse as she reached up and stroked Maxine's smooth cheek.

Her bare breast touched Maxine's and Maxine closed her eyes and drew a whispered breath. The wet silk of Maxine's calf and foot trailed down Regina's leg to her ankle. Regina loved Maxine's legs, she always had: those long muscled tapers that joined at a rounded ass and a tempting, trimmed wedge of ebony curls.

She trailed her fingers down Maxine's sides, resting them on her hips, one finger easing under the band of her bikini. She didn't realize she was holding her breath until her chest burned, and then she exhaled in a fast gasp. Was she still above water?

She squeezed her eyes shut and her voice barely rose above the breeze. "Max, I don't know what I'm doing."

Max's wet hand lifted Regina's chin, her thumb caressing along her jaw until Regina opened her eyes. "Honey, this isn't a test." Maxine's soft smile almost trembled but her eyes shone with empathy. "You have a beautiful body, Gina, full and curved, so classic. Your face is like an angel, truly, and your eyes watch me and you give me the thrill of being desired."

Gina scoffed. "Max, you must be used to it. Les can't keep his hands off you."

"He's a man, Gina. It's different. His touch is thrilling. He's funny, smart and strong and he understands me. I know I love him, and I'm pretty sure he loves me. Sometimes I wonder how much biology draws me to men, or if it's just culture that tells me I should be with a man. I don't like it when I feel that way."

"And Les?"

Maxine's smile twitched. "Les isn't like the others. He's the man of my dreams, but I don't just dream about men. He knows that about me." She leaned in and touched her lips to Gina's, soft, full and silky, the caress a breath of paradise that blew away confusion.

With a wet finger, she traced the outline of Regina's left nipple, as stiff and sensitive as it had ever been. "The hard part is, with most women all I have are looks and longings and dreams." She leaned in again, kissing the top of Regina's shoulder, her satin lips sliding feather light to the pulse of her throat.

The pent breath exited Gina's body in a moan. She slid her hands down Maxine's back, loving the creaminess of her wet skin. "I've dreamed too," she whispered before her head fell back exposing her neck to Maxine's warm kisses.

Maxine's full lips brushed along her jaw and cheek, light and tender, then hovered over Regina's mouth for only a moment before she closed. Regina's lips parted tentatively as she met the kiss, then fully as Maxine's tongue coaxed her own to twine and twist.

Maxine's fingers cupped Regina's breast, her hands teasing the nipple, and then Gina's hand cradled Maxine's right breast, thrilling at the fullness, at the pebbled texture of her areola. Desire boiled in her and she didn't hesitate when Maxine's hand tightened on Regina's hip in response to the caress. Regina lowered her head, smoothed her lips along her wet breast until they met the nipple. Light, careful, she parted her lips around the tip, caressing it with her tongue, tasting, and thrilling at Maxine's soft groan. "Gina," she whispered, caressing her back with needy fingers.

Maxine shifted and slid her leg along the inside of Regina's, ending the stroke by pressing her thigh and moving her hips in a slow gyration that massaged Regina's pussy. The pulse between her legs resonated and demanded. She suckled at Maxine's breast as her hand slid beneath the thin string of Maxine's bikini bottom. She cupped the round ass she'd dreamed of for so long, loving how it flexed as Maxine moved against her.

Sensations overwhelmed Regina—the sweet ache in her breasts sending pulses of pleasure to her core, her clit throbbing with the steady pressure of Maxine's thigh. Maxine slid Gina's suit bottom off, and then she moved her leg and let her fingers slip into Regina's pussy, slowly circling her clit.

She gripped Maxine and pressed, moving against her hand,

needing more. She stroked Maxine's ass. Somewhere in her mind she wanted to do more, wanted to give more, but only the growing pulse in her pussy and blood existed.

Maxine's fingers played with the folds of Regina's sex, slipped through the gate to test her, then began the slow, deep stroking, in and out, steady and sure, as her thumb coaxed the clit. All Regina managed was to cling to Maxine as her hips matched the rhythm. The gyre of pleasure grew, the thrum in her body deafened, and as her nipple was pulled and sucked, and long slender fingers filled her again and again, Regina knew only the strokes and the sweet reaching oblivion that seemed so imminent, but maddeningly far away.

The building wall of pleasure towered over her, paralyzing her, then crashed down in one long, rolling orgasm that flooded her soul with an explosion of color, launching her senses on an ocean of divine ecstasy.

Their lips met in a kiss so tender Regina's throat tightened.

Her breath returned as she realized what had just happened. She scanned the banks of the quarry. A few people watched them, but they hardly seemed shocked. It was almost summer. They were in college. The possibilities were endless.

She rested against Maxine for several moments before Maxine kissed her again then grinned like a canary-filled cat. Hand in hand, they made their way back to shore, naked as nymphs, renewed by the water and what they shared.

Breathing softly, quiet as the water itself, they lay nude, side by side on the shore, Gina's thigh resting against Maxine's. Nothing might ever happen between them again, Regina knew, or perhaps everything might. For now, for this moment, the world turned in perfect balance and Regina felt whole.

THE THINGS
I CAN DO
FOR HER

David Erlewine

After weeks of writing messages never sent, I finally email Lauren Reynolds at 1:15 a.m. and ask her to lunch later in the week, "schedule permitting." She's a senior associate at my law firm, rumored to be up for partner later this year, her sixth. Lauren is only five seven in heels but seems taller than me. She has high cheekbones, brown eyes, long black hair and olive skin. Her nickname around the office is Ten because she has it all. Her breasts are firm but round, a little more than a handful. Her ass is full and always jiggles just the right way when she walks on by. Whenever she leaves a room, she leaves a heavy cloud of perfume in her wake and many panting tongues. Her beauty is only one of many things that make Lauren Reynolds seem larger than life.

A few minutes later, while I'm debating whether to retract the message, she replies, *Friday at noon, Center Club. Come by my office at 11:50.* I write back, *Wonderful!* and click SEND, immediately regretting the exclamation point. When I click on properties I see she's already opened my message. I'm such a loser. I stand and make sure my office door is locked, even though I know it is. Other than Lauren (way down the hall), none of the other associates are even here, let alone partners. I dig into my gym bag and toss my towel onto the chair. Then I sit down and spread my legs slightly. I get up and check the door again. Getting caught doing what I'm about to do would likely make me the first associate to be fired this year and getting fired means I wouldn't be able to see Lauren every day.

I close my eyes and picture Lauren's thick calves, big ass and high cheekbones as I stroke myself lazily. I think about burying my face between her perfect breasts, suckling her hard gumdrop nipples into my mouth, tasting and teasing them with my tongue. I hate Lauren Reynolds but I want her. I want her bad and I don't know why. I stroke my clit faster, slide lower in my seat and wish I had something hard I could slide into my throbbing pussy. Last week, she called me into her office for missing a court deadline. She closed her office door and called me an idiot who deserved to be fired. I was all but crying, nodding and saying how sorry I was for not getting the brief in on time.

Now, as I'm on the verge of coming, instead of her telling me to get out of her office, I picture her throwing me to the floor and making me lick her left nipple while she sticks her fingers into my ass and then stuffs them in my mouth. The whole time that fat pink tongue of hers, so pretty and wet, is licking my ear between insults. She is holding me down on the floor and telling me I'm going to love eating pussy. I tell her no but she is sliding up on me, over my shoulders, trapping my head between her thighs. She is smiling down at me. That's how I come in a big wet mess, imagining her slowly crawling up my body until her clit is directly over my eyes, and I'm breathing her in.

After I clean myself up, my body is still tingling and I decide to go home because I have a bad case of Lauren Reynolds I can't seem to shake. I finish logging in the day's billable hours, read Lauren's message one more time, spray my office with perfume, and drive home. To stay awake, I slap myself every few minutes, imagining Lauren's perfectly manicured hand doing it. A few blocks from my apartment, I'm no longer tired, but I slap myself again. This time, Lauren holds me by the neck giving me one of her looks while her hand has her way with my face.

When I get home, my fiancé, Carl, doesn't come downstairs. When I look in on him, he's fast asleep, snoring softly. I lock myself in the bathroom and sit on the toilet, my feet against the wall across from me, furiously rubbing my clit as I think about Lauren Reynolds, her wicked body, her wicked ways. I come again, quickly.

Carl doesn't grunt, let alone stir, as I slide into bed.

My hands keep shaking at lunch. Lauren says nothing to me. Instead, she checks her BlackBerry and makes a couple of calls to the office. I catch her staring at my trembling hands more than once. I catch her smiling. She enjoys the effect she has on me. When the waiter comes, Lauren says, "We'll have two Cobb salads."

I look at her then mumble, "Dressing on the side."

"I'll have mine on the salad," Lauren says, handing the menu to the waiter.

Before he's even taken two steps from us, Lauren shakes her finger at me. "Don't ever speak for me."

My face burns and I stammer out an apology.

Lauren takes a sip of her iced tea. "Yes, you are sorry."

As we wait for the salads, she grills me about my fiancé, asks if he's as bald as he looks in pictures, says how shitty his law firm is and demands to know how I ended up with him.

When the salads arrive, I push the little bowl of blue cheese dressing away from my salad and begin eating.

"You really hate blue cheese," she says. It's not a question. If we were in court, I might object.

I nod and smile.

"Enough to get fired?" Lauren carefully sets her fork down and dips her pinky finger into the little bowl of blue cheese. Then she holds it up in the air.

I look at her finger for a few seconds and then take a sip of my iced tea.

"Are you slow?" she asks quietly, her irritation shaping each word, confirming my worst fears about myself. "Lean over."

I realize what she wants. I lean toward her and open my mouth. She jams her wet, rank pinky between my lips, rubbing it up and down my tongue.

She leaves it there until I swallow.

This isn't how I envisioned my first time eating pussy. I'm on my knees and my nemesis's hands are gripping my head so tightly, I can't move my neck. Lauren says things like "Slower" and "Bigger licks." I hold my tongue out and follow her instructions to move it counterclockwise and then clockwise. As directed, I lick her clit quickly every now and then. My jaw aches, but I obey. Soon, Lauren is hissing at me to keep still while she grinds on my face. I taste her juices on my lips. As her breathing slows, she leans down and traces the edges of my lips with her tongue. "You might keep your job after all."

When I smile, blushing, Lauren laughs, gripping my ears, which are a bit larger than I'd like. "Come on, Dumbo, round two." I flinch at hearing my childhood nickname but give in to the feeling. As I try to ease the tension in my jaw, slowly massaging my face with my fingers, I wonder how many other associates she has used like this. I worry about what she'll do when she makes partner. Lauren releases her grip on one ear and smacks my ass so hard I bite the skin under my lip.

"Get working," she says, turning around and jiggling her ass in my face. It's the kind of ass I've seen in face-sitting videos, crushing men's and women's faces alike. She bounces it off my face and then pushes me to the floor. She sticks two fingers inside me. Then she sticks her glistening, perfectly manicured fingers in my mouth and then back inside my pussy again. Soon, I'm a quivering mess. She has me exactly where she wants me.

"You young associates are so fucking eager," she says, fluttering her tongue in my ear. "Stick your tongue out so I can fuck it."

Once again, I do as I'm told, thinking back to how this all began with inviting her to lunch. I don't know how I feel about that. She drags me by the hair to her couch, laying me out so the back of my head is pressed awkwardly against the couch's edge. She squats over me and for a brief moment, I admire the perfect tautness of her toned thighs.

"I hope you've been doing neck exercises. Oh, and if you ever screw up a court filing again, I'll have you hooking on the street," she says, coldly.

I look up and try to smile, hoping these types of jokes will eventually stop as I advance in the firm, as she makes partner, as she grows to appreciate the things I can do for her. She grinds the back of my head into the hard couch. All I can see, all I can smell is Lauren Reynolds. She gyrates over my face, every few seconds moving inches up so I can swallow some fresh air. Sharp bursts of pain radiate down my neck. Finally, she comes. She's louder and more extravagant this time. Her juices dry in a thin hard shell on my face. With one last rocking of her hips, she steps away from me, leans down and whispers, "Get out."

* * *

Three days later, Lauren emails me. "Your memo was due hours ago. Get down here."

My stomach drops and I scroll through my emails, the whole time telling myself I'm either losing my mind or she's just messing with me. When I get to her office, she locks the door behind me. "You ran track in college. That was on your resume, wasn't it?"

I nod.

She looks me up and down, judging me. "You look like a runner, flat as a board and no ass. You actually look like a guy." She laughs. "I can't be the first person to tell you that. Do you ever think that maybe your bald fiancé is secretly gay, being with you?"

She puts her hands on my shoulders and pushes me to my knees. She reaches over to her desk and then squirts something onto my forehead. It drips into my eyes. It takes a second for me to realize it's blue cheese dressing. As I'm processing that, I realize her skirt is on the floor and her round ass is inches away from my mouth. She squirts dressing in the cleft between those two perfect cheeks, backhands my face, then points. Moments later, I'm licking pussy. I can't smell anything other than blue cheese, and I can't tell if Lauren is as wet as she seems or I'm just not appreciating how much comes out of those little dressing packets. She puts me in a scissors lock, cutting off the air passage in my neck. I can't believe how excited I get. I want to rub my clit but my hands instinctively clutch her thighs to reduce the mounting pressure around my neck. She spins me over so that my head and shoulders are flat against the carpet. She kneels between my thighs and out of nowhere conjures a large black dildo, veined like a real cock. She waves it at me, tells me she's going teach me a lesson. Lauren slides the dildo along my pussy lips: up, then down. I raise my hips, urging her to penetrate me with her toy. She laughs, flicks a finger against the hard nub of my clit, sending a sharp wave of desire through me.

"Keep your eyes open and watch," she says.

I do as I'm told. I'm getting good at that. Without ceremony, she fills my cunt with the dildo. I'm wet, so it slides in easily. Lauren braces herself with one hand against my thigh, her nails digging into my skin. Later, there will be red indentations and I'll have to come up with some excuse for Carl. Right now, I hiss, "Harder," and for once, Lauren Reynolds does what she's told.

I forget about the pain in my neck when I come.

The next Saturday, I'm at the office late but getting ready to head home for dinner. Carl and I are supposed to go out with another lawyer couple he likes. I shoot Lauren an email to say I'm taking off. My phone rings almost immediately.

"I come and you can go," she says.

I hang up and check my appearance in my compact. I can feel myself getting wet, wet, wetter. I hate myself for it. I hurry down to Lauren's office, locking the door behind me. She closes the curtains. When she turns around, she's wearing a bald cap and glasses. The resemblance to Carl is slight but jarring. She laughs. I never was very good at masking my emotions.

"Spread your legs," she says in a deep voice. I do, and she spins me around, kicking my ankles, and plants my hands on her desk, pulling my fingers apart. She shows me the biggest dildo I've ever seen, bigger than the one she tormented me with the last time we had one of these little associate meetings. "Get yourself ready," she says. I take a deep breath.

Before I'm quite ready, I fall forward as she enters me. I yell into her hand covering my mouth. After a few minutes of steady stroking, the dildo stretching me wider and wider, Lauren pulls out and pushes me to my knees. I feel empty. I want more. She flops the dildo in my face. "Open your mouth," she orders. I obey. When it comes to Lauren Reynolds, all I know how to do is obey. She clasps one hand around the back of my neck, tapping the fat, bulbous head of the dildo on my lower lip, then slowly sliding it in and out, my jaw aching terribly as I open my mouth wider and wider to accommodate the girth of this foreign object. "Hold still and keep your tongue down," she says, going deeper with the dildo than Carl's dick has ever dared.

"Sometimes I'd love to be a guy," Lauren says. "I'd love to hold a cock up to your eyes and soak them in cum. I would do so many things to your pretty, pretty face with a cock."

After she comes, Lauren dresses immediately, back to business. I slide a finger inside my pussy and rub my clit gently with my thumb, wishing it was her fingers on my body, inside me, satisfying me.

She looks back at me. "Go home and let baldy get you off."

That's my cue. I limp back to my office. A few minutes later, behind a locked door, I stroke my clit hard, so hard I can feel my pelvic bone beneath my fingers. I come fiercely, disgusted and exhilarated by what I've become.

I TOLD A STRANGER ALL ABOUT YOU YESTERDAY

Vanessa Vaughn

I told a stranger all about you yesterday.

I told her everything. The way your bright lipstick sets off the soft brown of your hair. The way your adorable crooked tooth is visible, but only when you laugh. I told her how your delicate fingers fidgeted with your wedding ring when I hinted about my feelings. I also told her that, ever since, you'd acted as if I'd never even mentioned it.

The stranger looked me over as I talked. She crossed her legs and settled into her leather chair at the hotel bar, sparking a long menthol cigarette with a little silver lighter. She leaned her head back, blowing a plume of smoke into the air. I watched her fingers as she held the tip over the ashtray. I couldn't help noticing they looked delicate, too—just like your hands, but without the wedding ring.

She listened intently. Of course, I was paying her by the hour. She was expected to listen. This woman analyzing my ramblings was no psychologist, but I knew somehow that a woman in her line of work could do more for my sanity than a member of any other profession.

She ran her fingers absentmindedly through her hair as I talked. It was long and black. I had requested a brunette. Her hair wasn't exactly like yours, of course, not quite the right shade, slightly deeper in color. She didn't have your lips or that quirky innocent smile. Still, there was something about her that was compelling. She was intense. She looked a little like you, but in a darker, less wholesome kind of way, her expression just slightly rougher around the edges. The woman sitting across from me now could never really be mistaken for your sweet suburban self. She seemed like you viewed through a warped lens.

I liked it. Something in her insisted I keep talking. Something told me this one wouldn't fidget with her fingers and look away if I hinted at what I really wanted.

And what did I want? The truth was, even I wasn't really sure. For once, I had another woman's rapt attention, but I still didn't know quite what to say. I was nervous.

Irritation started to creep into my voice as I spoke about you. I talked about the way you commanded attention every time you walked into a room. I didn't mention it out loud, but I couldn't help thinking about what a tease you were, how frustrating it was to want what I couldn't have. After all, I was tired of always being the pursuer. No matter how delicious you were to look at, I was tired of always being the one watching *you*.

Even though I didn't say all of this, somehow she still understood. "Follow me," she said; without questioning, I did. She walked to the elevators, cruel heels clicking loudly against the marble floor, and waited. I walked up next to her, wondering why the button hadn't been pressed. For a long moment, she didn't move, so I pushed it for her.

The doors opened, and we both entered. "Four," she insisted. I obeyed. Without a word, I reached out and touched the number quickly, watching it illuminate.

When we reached the door of the hotel room, my heart was pounding. Until now, this had all seemed theoretical, just a fantasy. Now I found myself assaulted by it from all sides. I smelled the fresh linens that had just been turned down. I noticed the slightly cooler air in the room, and the barely perceptible hum from the vents.

This hotel was nice, first-class. Still, I couldn't shake the feeling that these walls had never witnessed a pairing quite like this before. I knew that was ridiculous, of course. This five-star hotel had seen its share of salacious encounters, like any other—maybe even more—but I felt self-conscious.

The stranger walked into the center of the room and turned. I felt my stomach roll as she said only one word. "Undress."

It was a simple command, but it suddenly seemed complicated. I looked at the curve of her hips and her soft feminine lips and wanted to reach out to her, but she was watching me expectantly. Should I take off only my dress? Should I strip down to nothing? Should I do it seductively, watching her, or should I avert my eyes and obey?

In the end it didn't matter, really. My dress found its way to the floor and I found my way onto the wide bed. "On all fours," she said quietly. It took a moment to digest what she was saying. This wasn't exactly what I had in mind when I pictured my first night with a woman. I imagined you, of course—the blush of a first kiss, the slow awakening of passion. I pictured you finally noticing me as we sipped coffee together in your kitchen, or both of us overwhelmed by our desires as we rode together in your car during a storm.

What was happening here wasn't like that. This was no

date, and I didn't really know this woman at all, but the strange anonymity I felt now was thrilling.

As I raised myself up on all fours, facing away from her, I wondered what she had in store. I wondered how I should react. Surely more was expected of me than just this. What would she think of me if I didn't speak at least a little? I sat up and turned my head. "So what comes next?" I asked, trying to ease some of the tension. I was startled by her response.

"No questions," she said firmly, sounding surprised I had dared to say a word. I sensed her stepping all too close to me. And then it happened. Somehow, I heard the sound before I felt it. It was a jarring noise that seemed out of place in the stillness of the room, like a book dropped in a quiet library. I jumped at the noise before I realized that her hand had connected with my backside to produce it.

I felt only a mild sting at first, but then she slapped me again, harder this time. "What are you...?" I started to ask, but she quickly cut me off.

"I told you," she said with an air of finality, "no questions." Her blows came faster. They were swift yet precise, and she struck only in two places, leaving an exact mark on the highest point of each cheek. All of this felt strange. I thought seriously about interrupting as she continued. But then I realized that not having to speak felt like a luxury. I didn't need to be the aggressive one anymore. I didn't need to work for this woman's attention the way I always had to work for yours. I already had it. All I had to do now was obey.

I squirmed as she spanked me roughly, but I never really tried to get away. I didn't want to. After a while, I couldn't feel the sharp stings. Instead, a warm glow was taking over, the way a hand held against a cold window creates fog on the glass. A heat from inside me was creeping to the surface. I could picture my skin and the way it must look. I knew from the warmth that it was red and inflamed, but I loved the feeling. I gripped the bedsheets with my fingers. My eyes glazed over with a thin sheen of tears. But still I felt electrified by what she was doing to me.

When she stopped, it felt sudden. The blows had been so steady I was anticipating the next one with equal parts desire and dread. When it didn't come, I felt almost empty. I was eager for something more.

I felt her hands against the sides of my face as she pulled a blindfold over my eyes. She ordered me down onto my back, and I obeyed almost without thinking. I could feel the hot flesh of my backside soothed by the cool sheets. I could feel my lashes blinking against the smooth fabric of my blindfold. And then I could feel her fingers.

Suddenly I belonged to someone. This woman was dominating me, and I felt no need to resist. I could simply give in. She would satisfy me.

Then I realized you had nothing to do with this. It didn't matter if she had your precise shade of hair or your adorable crooked tooth. This feeling was what I really wanted, not you. I realized I was finally letting it happen. I was finally letting another woman in.

I said very little about myself that day. I hardly spoke at all. But yesterday I suddenly realized I was telling this stranger all about me.

CUT AND DRY

Heidi Champa

My heart skipped as Ida slid into the shampoo chair. Her perfume hit my nose and made my toes curl. I saw her every month, but the butterflies never went away. Her eyes were closed and she exhaled a deep sigh, but, she didn't seem to relax. The furrow between her brows told me something was wrong, just like last month. It was always something with Ida, but that was part of the fun.

"So, Ida, are you going to tell me what's wrong, or do I have to guess?"

"How did you know? I haven't said a word."

I pressed my fingertip lightly against the crease in her forehead, right between her eyes. The wrinkle disappeared and I felt her tension ease a bit. My breath caught as I felt her soft skin, but I tried to hide it.

"God, you are good. You are never going to believe it. That bitch was cheating on me. I told her, flat out, she and I were through. You don't think I made a mistake, do you, Karen?"

I shook my head no, like always. Each time she came in telling me she had dumped her latest conquest, I agreed with whatever she said. Ida treated me like most people treat their stylists. I was a confidante, priest and bartender all rolled into one. Most months, Ida sat in my chair, bemoaning her flat hair and unloading her emotional baggage. It seemed this month would be no exception. But each time she let a girl go I secretly said a prayer of thanks, a thank-you for making her single again.

"Anyway, that is the last time I let my sister fix me up. She wouldn't know my type if it jumped up and bit her. I will miss that bitch's tongue, though. She could make me come every time."

I let the warm water wash over Ida's hair. She sighed again and melted farther into the chair, her shoulders relaxing. Staring at her face as she enjoyed the sensations of the water made a moist heat start in my pussy. No other woman caused me to react that way. I always told myself I was as straight as an arrow, a perfect zero on the Kinsey scale. But something about Ida stirred my lust. I couldn't explain it and, it seemed, I couldn't control it. Pouring the shampoo into my hand, I paused for a moment before touching Ida again. I slid my hands into her hair, the lather foaming all over my fingers. I rubbed her scalp over and over, feeling her heat coming through against my skin. She moved again, this time uncrossing her lovely legs. Her skirt rose a bit, and her tanned knees peeped out from under the silky fabric.

"God, I should have you come to my house every morning. This is the only way to get your hair washed. Karen, you are magic."

I didn't answer; my voice was gone. Her lips were parted, and I could smell the sweet tang of cinnamon on her breath. I started the water again, washing away the sea of white foam. A stray drop of water moved over her forehead and slid down toward her neck. I watched intently as it rode a slow path over her skin.

My mouth was overwhelmed by the urge to lick it away. The heat in the shampoo room was suddenly thick. I could barely breathe. Ida's hand reached up and wiped the droplet away, but the trail of liquid remained, clinging to her soft flesh.

My mind wandered. I couldn't help it. I fixated on her smooth, soft neck where the water had just been. My fingers ached to touch her, slide over her hot flesh. As I moved my hands mindlessly through her hair, my eyes traveled lower to her chest and the two tight buds gently poking against the clingy fabric of her blouse. I closed my eyes, picturing the color and shape of her nipples. My tongue moved involuntarily inside my mouth, desperate for the chance to lick the stiff peaks that teased me during every visit. My fingers stiffened as my pussy flooded with heat, my imagination thick with visions of my hands on her firm stomach as I sucked hungrily on her nipples. My mind filled with thoughts of Ida, head thrown back, moaning my name in ecstasy as I teased her mercilessly. I was enjoying my little fantasy, until Ida's voice cut through my hot and hazy thoughts.

"You gonna wash all day, babe? I said I liked it, but this is a bit much."

Reaching for a towel, I tried to refocus on the task at hand, but again I found the feel of Ida's head under my hands distracting. No matter what I did, I couldn't stop envisioning her luscious breasts under my tongue. Again, her voice brought me back to reality.

"Earth to Karen. Where are you tonight? Don't tell me. Were you fantasizing about a new guy? Not that I blame you. While you were working those magic fingers, I was still thinking about that bitch and her tongue. I know I said it before, but I will miss that. It's such a shame she was crazy."

Ida sat, fixing her smock as she flounced into my chair. I stamped my foot on the pedal of the chair, raising Ida up a bit.

Mostly, I was trying to distract myself from thinking about Ida and her lover in bed together. My flushed face told me I wasn't succeeding. Ida didn't seem to notice, or she didn't care. Ida wasn't one to censor herself to protect anyone's feelings. Many a customer was left blushing by her racy stories.

"So, what are we doing to your hair today, hon?"

"Oh, Karen. I don't know. How about just a trim? What do you think? It just won't cooperate lately."

She looked absolutely beautiful with her wet, brown hair hanging around her face. Her blue eyes peeked through the fringe bangs I had given her three months ago. She stared at herself in the mirror as I let my eyes wander over her full mouth. Just as my gaze dipped, she licked her plump bottom lip. I forced my eyes back to hers, but she had caught me looking. A smirk of recognition crossed her face. She was used to getting looked at. I told myself my gaze didn't mean anything; it was just a passing glance. But I feared we both knew better.

"Whatever you want, babe."

"A trim it is. Why mess with perfection, right, Karen?"

Her last comment came with a wink, and I agreed. Perfection was the word for Ida. Ever since she first walked into my salon more than a year before, she had taken over my imagination. Every time I saw her name in the appointment book, my heart pounded. She showed up every month, always on time and always looking so beautiful. Her friendly nature made me like her immediately. She was one of the few clients who would ask me about myself. And while I wasn't as forthcoming as she was, I enjoyed talking to her more than anything. Her stories always managed to make me laugh, and moisten my panties. Her effect on me was growing with every visit. My confusion was starting to overwhelm me. Could it really be that I was falling for this woman?

My hands moved through her thick chestnut tresses, always so silky. I ran my comb through her hair over and over, watching the wet strands ease apart. I picked up my scissors and made fast work of trimming her hair while Ida filled in the details of her breakup.

"I came home from work early. Such a cliché, I know. I heard that bitch moaning all the way downstairs. She always was a screamer. Well, I went straight upstairs and threw the door open. And, there she was, in bed with a dude. A dude! Do you believe that?"

"Nothing shocks me anymore. Especially when you're doing the storytelling."

She smiled at me and my insides melted a bit more. It was amazing how after all this time she could still make me feel like a silly schoolgirl with just a smile.

"Fair enough. But at least with me you are never bored. Come on, admit it. You live for our appointments, don't you? You love me."

My head snapped up and we locked eyes in the mirror. She hadn't meant it to be a provocative statement, but as she stared at me, it sure felt provocative. Her left eye fluttered closed in a sensual wink, a trademark of hers I adored. I felt the jolt of it right through my cunt. The involuntary clench startled me with its intensity.

"You do tell some good stories, Ida."

She smile again and picked up a magazine. I tried my best to go back to work, but her words stuck with me.

All too quickly, I finished with Ida's hair and removed her smock.

"Well, what do you think, babe?"

"Oh, Karen. It looks beautiful. I love it. Once again, you have made me look fabulous. Hey, I have an event next week, would you be able to sneak me in first thing in the morning, just for a quick style?"

"Should be no problem. Just tell Angie at the desk what day."

"Great. See you soon, Karen."

With that, Ida walked out the door, pausing just long enough to give me a quick wave. As soon as she was gone, I ran up front to the appointment book to see what day Ida would be returning. Next Thursday. Just over a week and she would be back in my chair.

Thursday finally arrived. My week of waiting had driven me to distraction. I couldn't get Ida out of my head. I got to the salon early, hoping to have some time before Ida arrived. When I pulled into the parking lot, I saw Ida's black BMW waiting. Straightening myself as best I could in the car, I stepped out into the chilly morning air. Ida wore a business suit and big sunglasses. She walked toward me in very high heels that made her long legs look even longer.

"Thank you so much for doing this. We have this big presentation today, and I really want to look good."

"Leave it all to me."

I tried to keep my hands from shaking as I unlocked the door. Ida hung her coat on the hook and removed her suit jacket. The silk camisole she had on underneath clung to every inch of her. It was clear she wasn't wearing a bra, and her nipples peaked in the cool air of the shop. I threw on the heat and she followed me into the shampoo room. I swallowed hard as she sat down, pushing her chest out slightly as she eased her head back in to the sink bowl.

"Sorry to put you through this so early."

"Don't worry about it. It's my pleasure."

"Isn't it supposed to be all about my pleasure?"

She giggled, but my laughter died in my throat. I tried to keep my composure, but her teasing seemed more pointed than usual. I turned on the water and hurried through the hair washing. I was determined to be businesslike. But, as Ida sat up with the towel on her head, she hit me with another zinger.

"I wasn't expecting a quickie from you. You are usually so thorough. Must be all that sex with men. Over before you know it."

I watched as she stalked toward the chair, her hips swaying more than usual. It was like she was deliberately trying to work me up. If I didn't know Ida better, I'd say she was trying to seduce me. I ran my fingers through her wet hair, shaking her head slightly as I fluffed her strands out between my fingers.

"God, I love it when you do that. It feels so good. So, Karen, you didn't say anything last week. Are you seeing anyone?"

"Not at the moment."

"Why not? You're not still hung up on that Mitch guy, are you?"

"No. It's not that. I just, well, I haven't had much luck lately."

"Maybe you just aren't looking in the right places. Sometimes you find people in the places you least expect."

Ida swung the chair around so she was facing me. My eyes stole down and looked at her perky breasts in her camisole. Again, her nipples were hard against the pink silk. She grabbed my wrist and pulled me closer, her face inches from mine.

"I don't have a presentation this morning. I just wanted us to be alone, Karen. I've waited long enough for you to make the first move. You do want me, don't you, Karen?"

I stumbled to find the words, the thoughts, anything to make sense of what she was saying. My body was screaming at me to make a move, but something in my brain stopped me. The good girl, the nice, straight girl inside me was protesting. Ida reached up and touched my cheek, successfully quieting my inner prude for the moment. I swallowed hard, and somehow found the courage I had never been able to find before.

"Yes. I've wanted you since the first time you walked in here, Ida."

Ida ran her thumb over my bottom lip, causing a small moan to escape my lips. Her sleek, long fingers trailed over my face, leaving heat streaks over my skin. I eased closer to her, trying to bring our lips together.

"I knew it. I always knew it."

Ida touched her lips against mine, gently rubbing her soft, full bottom lip over mine. She stood up, moving me back against the wall without touching me. Her hands ran through my hair for a change, my blonde locks moving easily through her fingers. Suddenly, she grabbed a handful and pulled me to her. Our lips crashed together, finally fulfilling my fantasy of tasting her mouth.

Her tongue was hot, burning against mine as her hand pulled a little harder on my hair. I squealed, but the sound was trapped between our mouths. My hands instinctively moved to her barely covered breasts, rubbing the silk over her tight nipples. She released my hair, easing her hand down to my neck. Her nails gently scratched over my skin, as her tongue plunged farther into my mouth. She pressed her chest into my hands, and I obliged her by pinching her nipples between my fingers. It was her turn to moan, our mouths parting long enough to let it echo through the room.

My hand moved to the zipper of her wool skirt. I wanted to taste the rest of her, feel her wet pussy on my tongue. Any inhibitions I had were gone, replaced with the pure need to experience

Ida, feel her near me. I eased her skirt down her hips, wanting to prolong the anticipation. I stared into her beautiful eyes as I dropped to my knees in front of her. Her pussy was visibly wet, her silky panties clinging to her swollen lips. My hands trembled as I reached for her, my finger hooking on the elastic. I gasped when I pulled her panties aside and saw that her perfectly smooth lips were indeed slick with moisture. Her hand went to the back of my head, pulling me close enough to smell her strong musk. Tentatively, I slid my tongue gently between her lips, her sweet, tangy juices hitting my taste buds. My novice technique still managed to find her clit, hard and small under the tip of my tongue. A slip of a moan escaped her mouth, her hand clutching at my hair tighter. My finger eased inside her, her warm pussy opening to accommodate me.

I could barely believe it was happening, it all felt so surreal. My head swam and her moans filled my ears as I pressed on, slipping another finger inside her sweet, tight pussy. My tongue grew bolder, running up and down over her clit, no longer worrying if I was doing it right. Her body told me all I needed to know. Her hips thrust into my face, her hands twined in my hair. Ida was babbling, incoherent in her pleasure, my name tumbling out of her mouth, just like in my fantasy. I twisted my fingers gently as I pushed inside her, my tongue circling her clit over and over. As much as I wanted to touch my own pussy, I resisted. My focus stayed solely on Ida. I could tell she was getting close. I sucked her clit gently between my lips. Her pussy tightened around my thrusting fingers. She screamed.

"Oh, Karen. Keep going, just like that. I'm going to come."

Her hands were like steel on my head, holding me tight as she rode my tongue and lips. Her orgasm rippled over my fingers, a fresh wash of moisture coating my skin. Slowly, Ida began to stop moving, her hips jumping forward in one last thrust before falling back against the wall. She loosened her grip, her fingers gently caressing my locks again. With one last flick of my tongue, I pulled back and looked up at Ida. Her spent body rested against the wall, her thighs still visibly trembling. She pulled me up to my feet, her mouth covering mine before I could say a word. Her fingers rubbed my pussy through the denim of my jeans, making my desire acute and achy.

The button of my jeans was soon open, the zipper slowly lowering. But, just then, the front doorbell rang out in the silence. Ida and I jumped apart, straightening ourselves as my coworker Tim came into the salon. I yanked my pants closed, Ida zipping up as Tim's footsteps grew closer.

"Hey, you two. Early start, huh?"

Ida was back in the chair, looking innocently at a magazine. I knew my face was bright red, but I tried to ignore it, and the more pressing heat between my legs.

"Yeah, you could say that."

I was so relieved when Tim rounded the corner without another word. I turned to Ida, who just smiled. Picking up my blow-dryer with a sigh, I finished Ida's hair without another word. I could still smell her on my face; my mind was still stuck between her thighs.

CECILY

Kris Adams

Cecily sighed as she watched the movers load her furniture into the van across the street. Tomorrow her husband would be back to drive them across the country to their new house. She'd seen it in a photograph. It was newer and larger than their current home, but something about it left her feeling cold, empty.

"Did they get everything?" Cecily turned from the window and nodded sadly at Mary, her neighbor and dearest friend from the moment they first met two years ago. Mary wiped her hands on her apron and sat down at her kitchen table. "I can hardly believe that tomorrow morning Cliff will be here and…you'll be on your way. Did he say what time?"

"Around ten." Cecily walked around the kitchen, opening cabinets and inspecting their contents.

"You're making me nervous, Cec! Please, sit down. Tonight I'm making your favorite pot roast with red wine, and for dessert—homemade blackberry cobbler!"

"Oh, Mary. You don't have to go to all that trouble for me."

Mary smoothed her apron over her short dress. "Of course I do. It's your favorite and it's the last time I'll get to make it for you."

"Don't say that." Cecily laid a hand on Mary's wrist. "We'll visit, won't we?"

Mary cleared her throat. "You'll be nearly three thousand miles away."

"I just thought that...never mind." Cecily looked out the window. When Mary saw the distance in her eyes, she grasped Cecily's hand and squeezed.

"Of course we'll visit. What's a whole continent between friends?"

"Best friends," Cecily whispered. Her eyes were wet.

"Do you miss your husband when he's out of town?"

Mary sipped her wine before answering. "I used to. When we first got married, and Bill would be away for work, sometimes for months at a time, I'd cry myself to sleep. I was so lonely." She took another sip, licked the sweet wine from her lips. "Now it's not so bad. I guess I'm used to it."

Flipping through a box of photographs, Cecily found a picture of the two of them at a backyard barbecue, posing like high-fashion models. "So, what changed?"

"You moved here. I wasn't so lonely anymore," Mary replied. They shared a shy smile, and then Mary stood and pointed toward the bathroom. "You want the bath first?"

"No, go ahead. I'm taking this photo, okay?"

Mary leaned on Cecily's shoulder as she inspected the picture. "Oh, I love that one. You're always so glamorous. You could be a movie star." Laughing, Cecily reached up to thank her friend by softly stroking the hair at the nape of her neck. Mary sighed and kissed Cecily on the forehead before heading to the bathroom. "Take whatever pictures you want, honey."

"I will." She wondered if Bill would miss the photo of Mary in a racy two-piece bathing suit, winking flirtatiously at the camera. "Too bad," she whispered as she pocketed it.

"I'm coming in!" Mary peeked inside the candlelit bathroom, and seeing that Cecily was up to her collarbone in bubbles, she tiptoed in with a fresh glass of wine.

"Are you trying to get me drunk, Mary?"

Mary nearly tripped into the bath. "Of course not!"

"I'm kidding!" Cecily grabbed the glass and took a long sip. "Thanks. Oh, I must have forgotten to pack a nightgown. Do you mind if I borrow one of yours?"

"No, I don't mind." Mary couldn't help smiling. "You all set in here?"

"Yes. Sit with me for a while?"

"Sure." Mary sat carefully on the bathtub edge. They stayed silent for a while, watching the candlelight flickering, until Mary looked down and saw that the bubbles had started to dissipate. "Want some more bubble oil?"

"No, but can you do me a favor and get my back?" Mary knelt on the floor, took the washcloth and rubbed gentle circles over Cecily's shoulders. Careful not to wet her pinned-up hair, she squeezed warm sudsy water on her neck before scrubbing down her back. "That feels so good, Mare."

"N-nothing like h-hot water to relax you."

"It's not the water. It's you." Mary froze, and Cecily tensed, sputtering, "I mean, uh, you've got such a soft touch. That's what I meant."

"Right. Finished with your back." Mary rushed to her knees and grimaced at the wet spots on her robe where the water splashed. "Enjoy the bath."

"I'm done now," Cecily murmured, standing up before Mary could turn away. Mary's heart started to race when she caught a glimpse of Cecily's naked wet body, and it continued to race as she rushed back to her bedroom to look for a spare nightgown. She had only two clean gowns—one long sleeved and thick, the other sheer and short. She started to leave them both out so Cecily could choose; then she thought about tomorrow morning, when Cecily's husband would take her away forever. Snickering, she shoved the thick nightgown back into her drawer.

"Are you sure you don't want to stay in the guest room? You'd have a bed all to yourself."

Cecily turned down one corner of Mary and Bill's bed. "Why make up the guest bed just for me? I don't mind sharing if you don't."

"I don't mind. Just thought I'd offer."

"Do you have any lotion?"

"In the bathroom." Mary watched Cecily turn around, the thin nightgown barely concealing her slinky panties and lack of bra. Pulse quickening, Mary threw off her robe and slid into her side of the bed wearing a nightgown that was longer, but no less sheer than the one she loaned Cecily.

"This smells nice. Here." Slipping into the bed hands free, Cecily took Mary's hands in hers and rubbed. Mary smiled bashfully but didn't take her hands away, enjoying the gentle massage. "Give me your feet."

"Oh, no!"

"They're clean. C'mon." Ignoring Mary's protests, Cecily dug down into the sheets until she found a foot. "There. Move over." Rolling her eyes, Mary turned to lay her feet in Cecily's lap. "Don't you love to have your feet rubbed?"

Mary shifted nervously. "Bill rarely touches my feet."

"Same here. Cliff hasn't touched my feet once in the five years we've been married. The only hands my feet have ever felt were my own." She rubbed each toe individually, then ran her fingernail up the bottom of the foot.

"Ah! I'm ticklish!" Mary squealed as she pulled her feet back to her side of the bed.

"Sorry."

"No, it's fine." They stretched out, looking up at the ceiling. "What time is it?"

Cecily looked at the clock on the nightstand. "Almost eleven."

"We better get to sleep. You've got a big day ahead of you."

Minutes went by, but neither woman seemed tired. If anything, they were vibrating with nervous energy. Eventually Mary whispered, "So...what else hasn't Cliff done in five years?"

Cecily laughed, to her friend's relief. "The usual—cook, clean, pick up his laundry, remember my birthday, that sort of thing."

"I hear you there." Mary shifted nervously. "But...you love him, right?"

Cecily took her time answering. "Sure I do. Just like you love your husband, right?"

"Right."

"But that's not the only kind of love," Cecily stated quickly. "It's not like the love you have for your parents or your siblings. Or your friends." Mary nodded, her eyes trained on the ceiling. "I mean, I love Cliff. But I also love my friends."

Mary rubbed at her face to cover her satisfied smile. "I love my friends, too."

"Right. I mean, husbands are fine, but they can't take the place of a good friend. Someone who knows you and accepts you and treats you like an equal."

Mary turned on her side and looked at Cecily's profile. "Don't worry, Cec. You'll make tons of new friends in your new town."

"I don't want tons of new friends," Cecily spat petulantly, turning on her side toward Mary, "I want you."

Mary lost her breath for a second. "Oh."

Cecily groaned and slapped her hand down on the bed. "What am I gonna do without you, Mare? I see you every day. I'll be miserable."

"I know you have to leave," Mary sobbed, "but I don't know how I'm gonna let you go." They met in the middle of the bed, crying into each other's shoulders as they hugged tightly, like they were never letting go.

Cecily pulled back to look into her friend's eyes. "I don't want to lose you."

"You won't lose me. I'll always be your friend, Cecily." Mary wiped the tears from Cecily's face, but they just kept coming. "I'll always be yours."

Cecily grabbed Mary's hand and pressed it to her lips. "Mine?"

"Yours." Mary slipped her fingers through Cecily's hair, bringing her closer. "I'm yours." Though Mary had fantasized many times about kissing her best friend, it was Cecily who closed the space between them, pressing their mouths together in an act of passion and desperation.

They stayed like that, arms tight and shaking around backs, kissing without tasting, inhaling without breathing. Finally Cecily pulled away and rolled onto her back.

"I don't know what came over me," she whispered, near tears again. She held her free hand to her mouth, and Mary eyed the fingers as they covered the soft flesh that she'd just kissed. Wanted to kiss again.

"Cecily. Cec."

"Forgive me, Mary." Cecily looked away, offering Mary a view of the large throbbing vein down the side of her neck. Mary suddenly felt the urge to lick it, bite it, like a vampire in those pulp novels they used to sneak and read as teenagers. She'd drink Cecily down, every last drop of her, flesh and blood, until she'd possessed her entirely, and Cliff couldn't take her away.

"Cecily, are you okay?"

"No," Cecily sighed, looking up at the ceiling. "I don't know how to do this."

"Do what?"

"Be with you...for just one night. One night isn't enough, Mary."

"You want to?" Mary whispered, barely recognizing her own voice. She figured Cecily would have to think about it for a while, like she'd been thinking about it—this night—ever since they found out they would be parted. Longer than that, if she was honest with herself. She knew Cecily was thinking about all the time alone they'd spent in friendly embraces, touching each other's hair and faces for no particular reason. She hoped Cecily had treasured those sweet, delicious moments as much as she had, that the arm-in-arm walks in the neighborhood and extended good-bye hugs had made Cecily's heart race like they did hers. Her eyes asked the question again, and she braced herself awaiting the reply.

Cecily let out a long breath, wiped her eyes and nodded. "Please, yes."

The come-hither smile on Cecily's face melted any reserve on Mary's part. She didn't even notice herself moving, and then Cecily was turning quickly and they were kissing again. This time it was only chaste for a few seconds, until Cecily opened up enough for Mary to feel the fullness of Cecily's lower lip between hers. Mary sucked just a little, and then Cecily squeaked in her throat, and Mary sucked a little more.

"Mare." There was a gravelly texture in Cecily's voice that Mary had never heard before. It was so unlike her, and Mary wondered briefly if this was what her friend sounded like in bed with Cliff. Mary pulled back and stared at Cecily's wide eyes and open mouth for a second. She held her breath—Cecily did, too—as she released Cecily's hair from its bun and pushed it away from her face.

"You're beautiful." Before they could exchange demure thanks and return compliments, Mary went for Cecily's neck, seeking out the vein, this time with her mouth instead of her eyes. Cecily hissed, and soon her leg was sliding possessively over Mary's hip. *She's so soft,* Mary thought as she smoothed her hands over Cecily's leg and kissed her neck. Never had she felt such smooth skin that wasn't her own. This reminded her of kissing the inside of her own arm back in her teen years, before boyfriends, before marriage, before sex. Sometimes when Bill was away, Mary missed the taste of a kiss so badly she settled for the back of her left hand, the right hand busy and angry between her legs. But her hand, her arm, Bill's empty pillow, or the tops of her own full breasts could not compare in lusciousness to Cecily under her lips, in her mouth. Her eyes flew open when she realized this might be the only time she'd ever have Cecily this close, with her, in her mouth. She nibbled the ear in front of her and whispered, "Can I take this off you?"

Cecily answered with a soft, "Yes," then whispered it again when her best friend's hand slid under her borrowed gown, stopping inches from her breasts. Her breath hitched, and Mary froze, though she didn't pull her hand away, just stroked the skin.

"May I touch your—" Mary wasn't sure what word she was

going to use. Thankfully Cecily kissed her, breathing an unintelligible answer harshly into Mary's mouth. In her excitement Mary's hand fumbled, the back of her fingers slapping loudly against the underside of Cecily's breast. "Sorry!"

"It's okay." Cecily pushed closer, arching her back so her breast easily filled Mary's open hand. "It's okay, Mare." She hissed as Mary gave her a soft squeeze. "Do that again."

"This?" Mary held back a smile as she cupped Cecily's breasts, holding them with her palm, leaving her thumb free to drag heavily across the nipples. Cecily took a few quick, sharp breaths, her mouth falling open like an invitation, so Mary took it. Kissing Cecily and caressing her breasts at the same time reminded Mary of the midday naps she sometimes had, between chores and making dinner, when she'd be so tired she would fall back into bed and doze, bra undone in the front, pillow squeezed between her thighs. She often imagined Cecily across the street in her own house, baking, vacuuming, or even in her own bed, missing her own husband, making her own sheets sticky. She never dreamed—though she always hoped—she'd get the chance to ask. "Cec. How long?"

Cecily's trembling hand was on the hem of her own gown, pulling it up to expose her breasts, as if the thin fabric did anything to hide them. "How long what?"

"How long have you, you know?" Mary kissed Cecily's mouth open, and they both moaned like they'd been burned when their tongues met. She suddenly couldn't wait for Cecily's slow hands. She pulled away far enough to swat at the nightgown straps, wishing she could just cut through them with her teeth. Cecily slithered down, her hands above her head, her knuckles knocking loudly against the wooden headboard.

"How long have I wanted to kiss you?" wheezed Cecily as she lay flat on her back, her legs slightly spread. She kept her arms still, her breathing coming faster as she watched Mary's gaze move from her wide eyes to her wet lips to her swollen nipples, then down to the silky underwear—the Saturday Night underwear. Mary recognized the panties from the day they both ordered a pair out of a catalog, giggling as they'd purchased a money order and filled in a fake name for the return address. They were black and sheer and just barely contained the curly hair between Cecily's legs. Mary held her breath as she ran her finger over the thin strap covering Cecily's hip and wished she'd worn her own red pair.

"Yes, I want to know." Mary drew circles on Cecily's lower belly before zigzagging down to play with the first, fine hairs covering the pubis. "How long have you wanted this, Cec?" Cecily parted her legs and tilted her hips upward. Mary gasped, imagining that, if Cecily was as wet as she already was, with that small movement the silky panties were pulling deliciously on Cecily's crotch. Mary whimpered, wanting to look, to press her head down and watch her best friend's vulva swell. The curiosity nearly got the better of her, and she had to stop herself from ripping the panties away, possibly scaring Cecily, and herself. Instead she worked on her own nightgown, sitting up so she could pull it over her head. Before she could turn back she felt Cecily behind her, breasts warm and comforting against her bare back.

"A long time," Cecily whispered as she reached around to caress Mary's breasts. "I think," she cooed, rolling the nipples between thumbs and forefingers, "maybe...since I first met you."

"Me, too." Mary dared not look down at Cecily pawing her, squeezing her nipples until they were so hard she could barely feel them anymore. She arched, away from the hard nipples scratching her back, into the possessive hands on her chest, hoping one of them would find its way down into her panties.

They were just plain panties, but Mary knew from experience that they felt terrific when pulled tight and rubbed against her clitoris. She turned so they could face each other, kneeling on the bed, hands roaming everywhere within reach. Mary felt light-headed. "God, Cec. You can't leave me."

"Shh, don't." Cecily held Mary's head still so she could better taste her, tongue making long, deep swipes into Mary's hungry mouth. "Just kiss me," she moaned, and moved Mary's hand from her waist down between her legs. "Just touch me."

"Yes." Even through the panties Cecily felt hot. Mary's hands shook as she cupped her, fingers pressing down to tease the blood-filled lips. She kept her hand there as Cecily fell on her back and pulled Mary on top of her.

"Take yours off, too, Mare."

"Uh-uh. Don't wanna move my hand." Mary punctuated that by dipping her hand inside to cup bare flesh and hair. She pressed, and exclaimed happily at the feeling of fleshy lips and moisture against her palm. Cecily cursed, something she rarely did, when Mary slipped two fingers down to the vaginal *introitus*. Just pressing the fingers at the opening, not even inside, was enough to make them wet. Mary pulled her hand away and looked at the glistening fingers.

"Fuck." Mary wanted to laugh at Cecily's sudden attack of sailor mouth, but she was too busy watching Cecily jerk her own panties off before grasping at the ones stuck between her legs. Once they were both naked, Mary collapsed on top of her friend, kissing her roughly as she rubbed a thigh between Cecily's legs. "Keep doing...I'm so hot for you." Mary stopped long enough to rub her fingers, damp with Cecily's secretions, over both their mouths. Cecily looked like she might cry as Mary reached down, spreading Cecily's lips to tease her opening again. "God. Inside. Feel inside me, Mary. Please—oh!" Her eyes squeezed shut, but Mary didn't have to fear that the middle finger she'd slid inside Cecily's vagina was hurting her. Cecily grabbed her with arms and legs, and Mary added her index finger. "Damn it," Cecily whispered, then shoved her tongue deep into Mary's mouth, kissing her so hard Mary had to pull away to breathe.

"Want you." Mary stopped briefly to taste Cecily on her fingers and to adjust herself between Cecily's wide-open thighs. Cecily took the opportunity to lift Mary's breasts to her lips, sucking at them greedily as she rubbed her wet genitals frantically against Mary's thigh.

"Shit. Aw...fuck." Mary wondered if Cecily cursed this much when she was with Cliff, if she growled and looked so delicious and smelled so sweet. This time when she slid two licked wet fingers inside, she used her thumb to seek out Cecily's clitoris at the same time, smiling proudly when Cecily shuddered and started to fall apart underneath her.

"I want to feel you...come for me." This was another of Mary's fantasies—Cecily spread apart, being fucked until she screamed and cried—and Mary could barely believe she was the one doing it, that it was her pounding into Cecily's wetness and rubbing her stiff clit, that it was her thrusting against Cecily's pussy. For a second she imagined the four of them, Cliff fucking Cecily's sex open, then leaving her to finish Cecily off with her mouth and fingers while Bill took her from behind. It was crazy, but now that she'd tasted Cecily, felt her body, her hardness, her tight insides, Mary's future fantasies would be that much more vivid. Spreading her legs wide, she pulsed against Cecily's thigh as she sank her fingers in as far as they'd go.

"Oh, I'm going to." Nodding mutely, even though Cecily squeezed her eyes shut, Mary quickly pulled her sticky fingers from Cecily's musk and went about rubbing frantically at her clit, not stopping until Cecily squealed her name and collapsed into shivers.

As Cecily caught her breath, Mary wondered what to do. She was used to Bill falling asleep after he finished, rarely asking her if she wanted more. Now she wasn't sure what to expect.

"Cecily? Are you—" Being flipped over onto her back was nothing new—Bill rarely let her be on top—but being flipped and spread and kissed roughly, expert hands stroking her sex, was something she was not used to. "Oh...oh." It was all Mary could utter as she watched Cecily suck on her nipples, tonguing them with the flatness of her tongue as she rubbed circles around her distended clit. Fingers in Cecily's hair, Mary watched Cecily's kisses move down, and she spread her thighs wide, hoping to God that Cecily would give her what Bill rarely would, and ineptly well when he tried. "Cec, if you don't want to...do that... then you don't have toooooooooooohhhgooooood." She tried to hold back, but the moment she felt Cecily's soft wet tongue lapping her clit, she was finished. She rode the orgasm out hard, thrusting against Cecily's mouth and fingers as if Cecily could ingest enough of her taste and scent to last her the rest of their lives.

They didn't move for a while, until someone whispered a faint, "I love you" into the night. Once it was echoed, they fell asleep embracing each other.

"You're awfully quiet, honey." Cliff laid a large hand on his wife's knee. She patted it lightly, but didn't answer, just continued watching the world go by from the car window. "I know you're gonna miss Mary. But you'll soon love the new place, right?"

Cecily shifted in her seat. Her dress was scratchier than she'd thought, and the lack of underwear was hard to ignore. But then she thought about Mary, and she smiled. "Yes, dear."

"That's my girl." Cliff drove silently until coming upon a red light. "Did I tell you I ran into Bill the other day?" Cecily didn't answer, too preoccupied with shifting in her bucket seat so the fabric of her dress pressed nicely against her labia. "Looks like he's getting transferred, too. And you'll never guess where."

Cecily clutched the armrest. "Bill's getting transferred to the same state?"

"Same state, same county, same town, I think. We'll all be neighbors again soon." Cliff watched his wife's lips part and her eyes sparkle. "Happy now, baby?"

"Yes. Very happy." Cecily gave her husband a big wet kiss on the cheek before going back to staring out the window. She crossed her legs, squeezed her thighs together, and fell asleep smiling.

THE LEOPARD-PRINT MENACE

Melissa Gira Grant

'm her lady, and she's bent into the smooth white sedan, some
street in Springfield throwing itself under her rickety heels in
offering. Lady's girl is soliciting, outside the police station, all
ripped fishnet and black patent purse. My girl's leaning out
with overflowing fingers, hands bearing pale yellow sheaves, her
Xerox missives: *$27 Million to Arrest Prostitutes? No New Jails
for Women!* "Please? Sir?" She wince-grins at the honks, inevitable, and just like no one told her to, defies the yellow line.

It's cold, February, all white. My boyfriend hangs back on
the curb, newer than any of us to the winter protest thing. We're
flanked by more of Springfield's finest—my girls in black, defiant
boots and leather. This is what Massachusetts vice looks like:
some of my best friends and lovers.

"Let me kiss your lady hands." She brings my cold hands up
to her mouth. That's when she named me.

* * *

She crashed right next to me, getting guerrilla on my unsuspecting little porno practicum, taking a place at my side and being so fucking smart. I'd been asked to "come and speak to the sex worker's experience" for a class, barely more than a student myself. I certainly didn't have the papers yet. I climbed up on top of the teacher's desk to avoid the podium and there she was, seated at my hand.

Afterward, we traipsed across snow in the winter sun—I had high-heeled boots, and she had on these little silver slides—to prop ourselves on piles of laundry and bent-up zines and crushed pills in a dark little dorm that neither of us belonged in, dropouts both. We were swapping tales of sexually transmitted woe and back-of-the-free-paper ad copy, and "Can you really get off with all that in the way?" "Is pussy-eating dead?" and "So you can make enough money off this town?" and yes, yes. Yes—and no, no need to scrimp on Saran wrap, even in these leanest of times.

She told me she hooked up with her pimp momma and the accompanying aspiring *anarcho lesbo ho collective* (which must be said with high camp and an upturned girls'-school nose) after quitting a lefty canvassing job the summer before. All you had to do was ring up one of those numbers in the back of the free paper promising *Body and Mind, These Girls Have it All* and when the woman on the other end asked if you read Michelle Tea, it was like activating some sort of secret baby dyke escort code.

I laid my ho drama at her breast, having emptied our college cow town's rather limited larder of cash opportunities myself, burning bridges at the nudie bars, modeling for everyone (except the much-rumored pothead who would plead to jerk off on your face for a box cover shot, a messy deceit), pulling my "personal" ad after Yahoo complained *(Petite pervy undergrad, 23, requires tutelage from a gentle mentor. Can you help me with my homework? Tenure optional, tuition required.).*

When I have to go I gather my things and I let her be the cool one and orchestrate the swap of addresses (her hotel for my group house, and our online journals, and my phone). We both promise to really. Really. Get together. Soon.

I lose a little gray velvet glove in the lecture hall and so I wait as one lady hand gets cold.

We never have a first date. We have a full-on fucking engagement.

On my bed, we lube our life stories with two bottles of wine before nary a strap-on comes down from the shelf. We are showing off the way femmes do for each other. Our being theory-head femmes, it's got an even deeper kink.

She examines my books and takes the best ones into the bathroom with her: *Memoirs of a Woman of Pleasure*, with irony; my course reader for The Politics of Sex, without. "Read the 'Imperial Leather' essay, it's brilliant!" I say through the door. She pauses only to take charge of my housemate's over-sprouted bread sitting out on the counter, butters up thick slices for me and for her. She's talking while she's eating and saying not nice things for her prowess as a ho while gathering sunflower seeds into little handfuls. "I'm a lousy bang for the buck. I'm really more of a vibrator, a sex appliance, a consumer luxury."

Going with her to get more cigarettes from the Dairy Mart—and you can tell I want her, because I smoke with her—our old-school wine-stained lips set off a volley with the guys hanging out front. Even in January in New England, drunk boys will cruise the lot there and strut as easy marks, but starriest among them is a queen who is famous to me for doing Dionysus in Little Richard drag in last spring's production of *The Bacchae*, and he seems impressed with us, our delicate and drunken steps and arms almost touching and laughing for real together for the first time from his glam.

We strip down to trashy undies in my room and overwork the dim lighting into digital shots for my camera of us doing our best impersonations of ourselves. She pronounces my legs "stripper haunches" and I get her in a series of images doing her perfect thinky come-on face, with the pout and the conjoined female symbol charm just underneath it. "Let's put these on your live journal!" she says and she and I get what proves to be our foreplay published online before either of us gets an orgasm in edgewise over the congratulatory digital chatter of friends, strangers and lovers.

"Don't you have a harness?" she asks, the requisite fondling and kissing starting to feel too cloying to match the night that preceded it. I let her ride me, reaching up when she pulls me, grabbing and holding her firm, just one of her tits. She asks when she dismounts, dildo in hand, "Can we update your journal again?"

One last post, and we go under the covers, until she gets too hot to be too close—never can stay the whole night until my last one with her, always gets the laptop or a book and nests with those at the edge of the bed when our bodies and the distance between needs broaching—and we go to sleep so wasted and still making sense, burned at the edges and preserved for posterity, sleeping the day away until we're next called to duty, at ease, entwined and ready.

THE BACHELORETTE

Julia Peters

When I hear there's a party of twelve, all women, for 9:00 p.m., I am surprised. This is a hundred-year-old steakhouse, and while things have changed in the last hundred years, we're not usually a destination for girls' night out.

"I hope they don't just order a bunch of salad and salmon. *White wine*," I say to my friend Alan, who is also assigned to the table.

"How sexist, Sage," he says. "Simone de Beauvoir would be appalled. So would Courtney Love."

"You have to download some music from this century," I say, hoisting my tray and heading back out to the floor.

As it turns out, these are Porterhouse and scotch kinds of girls, my kind of girls, at a much higher price point. It also turns out to be a bachelorette party, and I've seen the bachelorette in question in here before.

She's come in a half dozen times that I've seen her, with her boyfriend. At first I noticed her because the boyfriend is a bass player with a superfamous anthem-rock band that has managed to hold on for the last twenty-five years. She was, on any given night, one of the youngest women in here. She is also perfect, rock 'n' roll perfect, wearing diamond-and-skull jewelry and boots that nearly reach her hips. Her hair is glossy, long and black. She hangs on the bass player's every word, yet seems completely confident and royal. If girls like her came to my band's shows, I'd know we've made it. Three years in, I don't see the end in sight, or this tray of sirloins coming off my shoulder any time soon.

So here she is, about to marry the bass player, wearing a metallic purple minidress and giggling sweetly as she opens box after box of unmentionable underthings.

She looks phenomenal, as always. She says, "Thank you," in a demure whisper every time I give her something—a new fork, another Hennessey, an extra shopping bag for the presents. She looks up at me from beneath her eyelashes. She introduces herself as Sasha and says to let her know if they get too rowdy. They don't want anyone to be annoyed with them.

I'm used to getting hit on here, but by men. This is interesting. That is, if she's hitting on me.

"Your lady and her friends are not a complete nightmare after all," Alan says as we go over the bill together, three hours later.

"My lady? I don't even know her."

"Please. Every time she comes in here your tongue rolls across the floor like a red carpet."

I smile at him. "Okay, she's totally hot. But I'm straight."

"So far," he says.

They shut down the restaurant. My manager is unusually okay with this because they've thrown so much money around and managed not to piss anyone off. Tonight, Alan and I have made what we'd normally earn in a week. He and my manager leave. I agree to hang out in case the bachelorette needs anything. I'm also hoping to talk to Sasha, not that I know what I would say.

I'd usually sit at the bar and have a scotch with our mixologist, Brian, but I'm beat from working the party and don't need a drink. I go out the back to the loading dock area for a cigarette. This is an industrial area and it's usually pretty quiet and lonely out here.

The side door opens and Sasha struts out. I can see her shoes now, Louboutins with red soles, gold and death-defyingly high. She smiles.

"End of the night?" she asks, gesturing at my cigarette.

"Yeah. I was going to go check out my friend's band, but I think I'll skip it at this point."

"You play, right?"

"Yeah, lead guitar. How did you...?"

"You chatted with my fiancé once about his group. You sounded like you knew what you were talking about. A lot of girls don't."

"I don't know those girls."

Sasha rolls her eyes. "I do." I laugh. She walks over to me and takes out her own cigarette from a metal case, and I give her a light.

"Do you guys need anything in there?"

"We ordered espressos. Brian took care of it."

"Oh, shit, I'm sorry."

"No, no, please. We're keeping you here late and you guys were all so accommodating tonight. I really appreciate it."

I take a drag and nod. She takes a long drag and drops the cigarette, puts it out after a few puffs. She stands before me and I have the distinct impression I should put mine out, too. I stub it out on the brick wall next to me.

"So, congratulations. On your marriage."

Sasha laughs, low and throaty, the girlishness disappearing. "Thanks. He's making an honest woman out of me. Kinda."

"Kinda?"

"I love the guy. I really do. But we have an understanding. He travels a lot, which requires my understanding. And I...like to play. He is very understanding of that."

Her words are so well rehearsed. I wonder how many times she has given this speech, but I'm also getting very excited that I'm getting the speech.

"Really?"

She takes a step toward me. In her crazy heels she is about my height. "Really."

It's now or never. I run my fingers through her hair and she sighs a little. "And...uh," I glance toward the door. "How understanding are your friends?"

"Very. It is my night after all."

"Yes, it is," I say. Sasha puts her hands around my face and pulls me into a soft, luscious kiss. It is hot and off-putting at the same time. It's too gentle for me. But maybe that will change.

When she pulls away I say, "I should tell you I haven't done this before."

"Swinging?"

"Girls."

"Oh," she says. She sizes me up to see if I'm worth the risk. "But you want me?"

"Fuck, yeah. I'd have to be insane not to want you."

She likes this answer. "Show me."

"Come here," I say. She steps toward me, expecting a kiss, but I walk her with me back a few steps, behind a short wall, so we're out of immediate view of the street and the small window in the side door. I twirl her around so her back is against the wall and pin her shoulders with my hands. I take a long look at her, all of her, and then draw a long, rough kiss out of her.

She's out of breath when I let her go, panting. I drop to my knees. The concrete hurts, but I like something about that, about this whole scene. I reach under her dress and grab her ass, kiss her once through the dress, about where her pussy is, kind of a preliminary for myself. Then I pull her down on top of me.

There is absolutely no challenge in this dress. The V-neck ends at the halt of her rib cage. A little string across the back of her neck keeps it from falling to the floor. It is a rock 'n' roll dress, the dress of the woman who is with the band, the headliner, the one who fucked her way out of the groupie pit. Sasha does not need a bra, in the best possible way.

"Shouldn't you take me somewhere?" she asks. She looks shocked, a little ticked, but still turned on, so fuck it.

"Is that what your girls usually do?" I decide I'm not going to pull the little string that undoes the dress. That's what the string is there for, so it's a chump move. Instead I pull the top of the dress to one side, as rough as I can manage without ripping it. Not that she would care. Her breast is firm and small with a hard, dark nipple. I lick it once, roll it between my fingers as I continue to talk.

"They take you somewhere?" I get my hands back under her delicious little bare ass and pull her onto my lap. She inhales hard. I'm proud of myself for continuing to surprise this girl who has probably seen a lot more than I have.

"Well, I've never done this before, but I'm not one of your girls." I pull the back of the dress up to her hips. I run my hand smooth and quick around to the front and then between her legs. To my surprise there is soft silk there—I don't feel the waistband of the thong.

I move my fingers beneath her panties. There is the slightest brush of hair on her mound. She parts her legs a bit to let me feel her and to my relief she is very wet—relief because I really don't know what I'm doing, and if this girl wasn't hot for me already, I wouldn't know the mechanics of how to get her going. I tell my brain to stop thinking of this searingly hot girl like she's a math problem. My brain shuts the fuck up.

"And anyway, is it really going to be a problem if any your friends see you?"

She laughs soft and low and throws her head back. The unspoken answer is no, it won't. Her friends won't be surprised. They might even join us. I don't think she'd mind any of the restaurant staff either. No one is going to snap a picture, we're too discreet. I lean down and pull that beautiful nipple back in my mouth.

Sasha gets her hands on my thighs, beneath her own, pushes herself up and arches back to ride me. She is quick and light, moving up and down magnificently, like she took a class in fucking someone's finger. I turn my hand so my finger is curving slightly inside her and she comes down on my palm. I think about circling her clit or something but she's moving fast and I don't want to get in her way. Instead I cover her breast back up, then move the material aside from the other one and get to work on it with my tongue. I can feel her open lips and clit against my hand when she comes down on it. It's pretty amazing.

She moves her head back toward me and slows her movement. I come up from her tit. With one hand she pushes me back, then farther back, so I throw my free hand behind me to keep myself from falling. Sasha repositions herself a bit so she's now sitting in the palm of my hand with my finger completely inside her.

"Another finger," she says breathily. I do what the lady says. She moves back and forth, grinding with my two fingers inside her. They seem to fill her up. Now she's rubbing her clit against my palm. She moans breathily, little "oh's" coming from between her lacquered lips.

She looks me over briefly, appraising my buttoned-up white shirt and my bun, my black slacks and my shiny black lace-up shoes.

"Take your hair down," she says. She stops moving but flexes her vaginal muscles around my fingers. It's cool as hell.

There's no way for me to reach my hair without falling flat on my back. "You have to do it," I say. She takes out the barrettes and lets them drop. My blonde hair falls half out of its up-do. Sasha undoes the buttons on my shirt without asking. She yanks my plain beige bra, a work bra, down and my breasts fall forward.

"I going to come very, very soon," she says in this pouty, bad schoolgirl way. I bet that turns the rock star on. "I wanna suck on those big beautiful tits while I do. Give them to me, baby, please."

I think she likes it when she talks. Whatever, I like it too. She stays there, starting to move back and forth again very gently, so wet, restraining herself from working toward her orgasm. Oh, I get it. "Suck on my tits, Sasha." She moans and falls forward on them, both hands around them, and starts licking my nipples and sucking on them gently.

She starts to grind toward coming again and now those hot little "oh's" are muffled by my tits and she's singing "Mmm! Mmm! Mmm! Mmm!" into my body. This girl is all rock 'n' roll and entitlement, all flutter and perfume and tobacco. And I'm about to make her come. Right now, I feel like the rock star. I would tell her to say my name, but she probably doesn't remember it.

I can smell the sweet musk from her cunt, her overly sweet

perfume, and the smells of grilled steak and scotch and the musty, putrid street. I can smell my own sweat and hard work. It actually smells good.

She takes her mouth off me and puts her hands over my tits, furiously bucking now. It's an effort just to keep my hand in the right spot but I do it. She yells once, and I stop bracing myself against the dock with my free hand to pull her face to mine by her blown-out hair. She gasps but I think it's a good gasp—she keeps going. I should tell her to shut up but I'm loving this way too much at this point so instead I tell her, "Tell me I'm making you come. Tell me. Tell me."

"Oh, god," she sighs, close to my ear but not so quiet that it takes away from how hot this is. I'm still holding her by her hair, mainly to keep from falling over. "You're making me come, you're making me—oh, god!"

"That's it," I say, and start finger-fucking her again as she meets my hand with every thrust. "That's it, come for me, come on."

"Yeah yeah yeah yeah yeah yeah—oh! Oh! Fuck, I'm coming! I'm coming! Yeah! Yeah! Yeah!" She throws her arms around me and shudders and bucks and squeals as she comes. She is absolutely magnificent. My guess is she always comes.

Sasha is still moving, coyly shuddering now and then, when she drops one hand down to unbutton my pants. This isn't what I want exactly. I want Sasha in a bed sucking my clit and licking me to orgasm after orgasm on high thread count sheets, fucking me from behind with a strap-on while I look out at the city from a penthouse window, masturbating for me with her legs wide open sitting in a chair. I want us licking champagne off each other in a hotel room we've been in for days. It had never occurred to me to want all these things from her until this night. I don't really want a hand job in an alley as an afterthought.

Her aftershocks subside and Sasha pulls my hand out of her cunt. She takes my fingers and sucks on them as she winds both her small hands down into my underwear. Her taste seems to turn her on. I'm not surprised.

I'm as wet now as I was when we started. The long mani-cured nails of her one hand flick along the lips of my cunt, while the other hand finds my clit and starts working on it, jerking me with her fingertips ever so lightly. She starts putting her fingers inside me—they are so delicate that there are three inside me before I realize she's easily sliding in a fourth. I look at her. Her eyes are closed, concentrating on her fingers' rhythm, but also on her own; she's moving her hips in almost-violent circles like a belly dancer and running her tongue around my fingers in circles that match, turned on enough to make herself come again with barely any assistance from me.

I don't move. I'm in awe—of what I'm doing here on the loading dock where anyone could see me, of what I'm doing with this incredible woman, who I wish I could have and wish I could be. I'm in awe of the tornado that's ripping through her for a second time as she *ohhs* and *mmms* and grabs what she wants for herself again. I'm in awe of her expert fingers, of a technique she must have patented or something as she coaxes and teases and then at last pulls my orgasm out of my cunt, my clit, my sore feet and knotted shoulders. I laugh deeply as it happens. I laugh at how absurd this is. My clit practically glows, warmly spasming in a consistent, steady pulse. She keeps going and so do I. She finishes and opens her eyes to watch me laugh and twitch between her fingertips.

"You're a very interesting woman."

I don't know how to take this. It's a compliment in my mind, but probably not coming from her. She didn't say what a hot girl I was or anything. I realize what Sasha is about, and I could be about that for a while, but not for long. She withdraws her hand. I notice she doesn't taste her own fingers.

Sasha tilts her head toward me and shimmies her ass a little. "Do you wanna come with us to the party?"

I button up my pants and start working on the shirt. "This wasn't the party?"

Sasha moves the top of her dress over an inch to cover her breast back up.

She smiles. "Well, you certainly were, baby. But in there was just dinner. We're just getting started."

THE GIRL IN THE GORILLA SUIT

Lori Selke

It all started the night that she fell into my arms—literally.

I was front and center stage at my favorite club on my favorite night. Every other Friday night, Club Cameo threw a Disco Circus party. It was cheesy, but intentionally so. They'd throw up a disco ball, get the DJ to play anything bass thumping and booty twitching, and then on the hour, they'd do a little circus skit up on stage. Sometimes it was burlesque dancers. Sometimes it was clowns. Sometimes it was clown burlesque—I will never forget the girl who used red rubber noses as pasties and ended her act by honking them. *Toot, toot!*

Sometimes there were aerial acts. I loved watching these. When I was just a little baby dyke, my favorite activity in gym class was climbing the rope to the top of the rafters in the gymnasium. I loved to race the boys to the top, and as I was smaller and lighter and just as strong, I almost always beat them. So it was a special thrill to watch someone twist and turn—dance, really, with the rope as a partner—high above the club. I could imagine myself as the woman in the air, looking so graceful, flexible and beautiful. The patrons would stop dancing for a moment and hold their breath, faces upturned into the stage lights.

And then there were the odder acts, the ones that loosely fell under the rubric "freak show." They were just skits of high silliness, sometimes more successful than others. The girl who walked on broken glass—hot. The bearded lady? Strangely hot. The guy who yelled, "Human firehose!" before spitting his drink all over the front row? Not so hot.

The night I fell in love, it was an animal act. Some lovely long blonde thing was dressed as an animal tamer. Tall boots, tails and top hat—and red satin corset and short shorts: very nice. She had a series of performers in animal costume perform "tricks" for her: she turned a fierce lion into a purring pussycat; a man in an elephant mask (no trunk puns, fortunately) let her ride on his back; and then there was the gorilla.

She was a girl gorilla; you could tell because she wore a pink polka-dot bikini. She also sported blonde braids with bows to match her outfit.

She was also a naughty gorilla. The animal tamer offered her bananas, but she just stole them and refused to do tricks. Finally, the animal tamer grabbed the gorilla girl and tried to turn her over her knee for a spanking.

I think the gorilla girl was supposed to struggle and protest. I don't think she was supposed to struggle so hard that she slipped right out of the animal tamer's lap. The tamer had placed her portable folding chair right near the edge of the stage, so we could all get a better view of the mock spanking, so when the gorilla girl started to fall, she had nowhere to go but right over the lip of the stage and into the audience.

Which is how I suddenly found myself on a Friday night with my arms full of a girl in a gorilla suit, surrounded by applause.

I don't really know how I managed to catch her. All I know is that I was cradling her in my arms like a baby, the audience was roaring all around me and I was looking into her eyes. They were the only feature I could see. They looked both frightened and relieved. I lowered her carefully to her feet. She grabbed my face and "kissed" me—pressed her rubber lips to mine. It would have meant nothing, if not for what came next.

She pulled my head down to speak into my ear. "Thank you so much, you saved my life!" she said. Her voice was muffled by the mask, but I could still make out the words. It was husky, low, the kind of voice that always sounds like it's mocking you, but I could tell she was sincere (if hyperbolic) this time. She tousled my hair with her furry gloved paw, and then she was gone.

Except for her scent. There was the faint burnt smell of rubber, yes, but something else as well. Something muskily floral. I liked it. I wanted to smell it again.

But by this time, she was nowhere in sight.

I didn't know her name. I didn't know her face, even. I knew nothing at all about her except her voice, her scent, the feel of her body in my arms.

It was enough.

I tried to meet her after the show, but this was a club, not a proper theater; it didn't have a standard backstage door. Besides, I didn't know what she looked like. I went home alone. It was three in the morning. I was stone sober.

I dreamed that night of a polka-dot bikini trimmed with coarse black fun fur, and of burying my face in the creamy cleavage of the woman who wore it.

I knew I should just let it go, that I should just accept it as a chance encounter, a small gift from the universe—a girl in a gorilla suit, falling into my arms, a girl with a sexy voice and a seductive scent. Maybe all I was destined for was a chance to hold her for a moment and look into her eyes, never to know who she really was. Maybe I wasn't meant to know who she really was. Maybe I shouldn't tempt fate.

By the end of the week, though, I was having full-blown fantasies about the girl in the gorilla suit.

It didn't start out entirely intentionally. I have a method I use when I'm spending quality time with myself. I like to jerk off just before bed—it's my favorite way to relax after a long day, and the best way to guarantee a good night's sleep. Plus, I'm less grumpy in the morning. I start out by just rubbing the tops of my thighs and my mons gently. While I'm warming up like that, in my head I like to sort through a wide variety of mental images, like cards in a deck: an old memory fragment of a lover pinning my wrists to the mattress, or how a sexy friend of mine looked when she bent over in a short skirt. Or maybe a scene in a movie, or a picture in a magazine. I just run through them over and over in my head until I find one that makes me gasp. Then, whatever triggered a reaction becomes the basis of my fantasy for the night.

One night, it was the memory of her falling off the stage, into my arms.

Somehow, it quickly morphed into a different scene entirely. My mind is like that sometimes. She was no longer in the full suit; she just wore a rubber gorilla mask, and that polka-dot bikini, but instead of fur there were her bare limbs, pale and unadorned. She did a striptease for me, losing first her top, then her bottom. She presented herself to me proudly, arms spread, completely naked from the neck down. Nipples erect, dark pubic bush gleaming with a hint of wetness. Finally, her hands lifted to her face, grabbed the edge of her mask and started to pull it off—

—and that's when I came, hard, and much sooner than I expected, all in a gush.

Soon I was imagining all sorts of things, every night: a woman in a gorilla mask, tied spread-eagled to my bed. Did I dare lift the mask? I did not. Instead, I buried my face between her legs. Engulfed by that beguiling scent, I licked and suckled her clit until she pinned my head between her legs and wailed, her cries muffled beneath rubber and fur.

Or I pictured myself helping her zip up backstage, the zipper getting caught—putting my hand down the back of the suit to help free it, slipping farther down, farther...

Or I was watching her fellate a banana, then force me to eat it while she held it to her crotch—onstage.

Finally, I even started daydreaming. We would go out on a date, to an art gallery. She would be wearing her mask. The gallery owner would mistake her for one of those art provocateurs, the Guerilla Girls. I would have to explain that no, she was just my girlfriend. She would laugh behind her mask, and we would stumble out into the night, arm in arm, toward my apartment and endless domestic bliss.

Two weeks later, I was at the lip of the stage again.

I didn't really know if I would see her again, that night or ever, but I figured it this way: if she'd invested in a full-blown gorilla suit, not just a mask, the odds were in my favor. Of course, it could have been a rental suit. I knew that, too. I kept my fingers crossed.

I also came prepared. In my back pocket was a note with my name and phone number. *I'm the girl who caught you in my arms. Call me?* I wasn't entirely sure what I was going to do with the note, but I could figure that part out later.

Late in the second half, my bets paid off. There she was, all suited up, and dancing. She was doing some mockery of urban tribal belly dance—her gorilla suit was complemented this time by some braids made of yarn and cowrie shells, and instead of a polka-dot bikini she wore a studded belt, bell bottoms, and jingly bra.

Except that she was far too graceful to pull it off. When she shimmied, and those coins shook, I felt woozy. And I wasn't the only one: the audience was silent, rapt.

Then she leaned over the stage and shook her cleavage in the face of the woman standing next to me, who screamed with delight and stuck a dollar bill in the band. And I had an idea. Hastily, I wrapped my note inside a dollar bill of my own, and waved my hand in the air.

Just before she turned and wiggled her furry ass at me, did she make eye contact? Did she wink? Or did I imagine it? I tucked the note and the bill into her fancy leather belt. My hands were inexplicably shaking, but I managed to make sure the bundle was secure.

Then I headed to the bar in the back of the club and ordered myself a whisky sour. I didn't normally lean on liquid courage like this, but tonight, I needed something to drown the butterflies suddenly taking flight in my stomach.

I waited until the end of the show, when the lights dimmed over the stage and brightened over the audience, and the DJ climbed back into the booth to play one last set before last call. No one winked at me on her way out. Nobody offered a shy little wave of hello. There was no sign that the woman beneath the gorilla suit had gotten my note, or read it, or wanted to know more. I waited until closing time, nursing my drink, until they shooed the last stragglers out into the eerily silent streets.

Nobody called me that week. Or the next week.

Not that that stopped my fantasies. I imagined her pulling my head back for a rubber-lipped kiss; spanking me with rubber-gloved hands. Once I dreamed of her dancing in the ropes just like the aerial acts I loved, naked, with her mask on as always.

Once I dreamed of lying on my back onstage while she did the splits above my face.

Only now for some reason, sometimes, when I came, I found myself with tears in my eyes.

Of course I went back for the next show. I didn't have a note. I didn't have a plan. I just had a threadbare hope of seeing her again onstage. Even if she didn't call, I wouldn't mind watching her perform again. I liked how she moved, and I liked her sense of humor—and her voice, and her smell. And if that's all I ever had of her, it would be enough. Eventually I'd find another set of fantasies to get my juices flowing and my fingers flying.

The first half ended without any sign of the gorilla girl's act.

I could feel my heart sinking toward my shoes. I knew I was being ridiculous. I took three deep breaths and headed for the bar.

I was waiting for my whisky sour when someone brushed a hand across my shoulder. I didn't even look, just slid a few inches over to make room for whoever was next in line. I kept my eyes fixed on the bartender and the tattoo of a crown at the nape of her neck—nice—so I didn't see at first who it was who was leaning in to whisper in my ear. "Hi," said a low, smoky voice that tickled at my memory. "Nice to see you again."

I narrowed my eyes in suspicion as I turned. The voice was familiar but the face was not—round and brown and definitely cute, with dark red lips and eyelashes for days, and a cute little pixie cap of jet black hair, with spit curls near her ears. Cute, but a stranger.

But my mother taught me manners, and I tried to be warmly polite as I asked, "I'm sorry, have we met? I must have forgotten your name."

She smiled and looked down, into her drink. "Well, it's hard to explain. You wouldn't recognize me, but yes, we've met before. About a month ago, I think." Her look turned playful. "You caught me." She gestured at the stage.

My eyes widened. "Are you...?"

She laughed. "The gorilla girl. Yes. My name is Mona. Thank you for saving me," she said, and leaned over to kiss the back of my hand. I giggled inanely and covered my mouth with my hand, embarrassed.

"I'm sorry I didn't call you," she said. "I guess I'm a little shy. I wanted to introduce myself first, here, at the bar. Just in case, you know?"

"In case of what?" I asked.

The club was too dark to see if she was blushing when she answered, "In case you changed your mind."

And suddenly I liked the girl out of the gorilla suit just as much as I liked the girl inside the suit. I knew neither of them. But my chance had finally come to get to know them both. "Let me buy you a drink," I said to her, "and let's see how things go."

THE OUT-OF-TOWNER

Delilah Devlin

Maybe I felt the unexpected attraction because we had been
forced to share the same hotel suite. Or maybe it was just
the late hour and I was bored. All I know for certain is when
I put down my red pen after working diligently on notes for
revising my portion of the proposal, my gaze caught Debra's
breasts.

Her sudden exhalation drew me to the shadowy cleft revealed
by the two buttons she'd undone at the top of her blouse.

Already I could see the full, round curves as they pressed
close together thanks to the magic of underwire. I stayed trans-
fixed by a little shell button, turned sideways in the buttonhole,
ready to pop free with her next deep breath.

I realized I'd been staring, and so far she hadn't noticed
because her own attention was focused on the colorful charts
spread in front of her. "They're crazy, you know," Debra said,
as she tapped one chart in particular. "How the hell are we
supposed to find fifty thousand to scrub from this estimate?

We've already cut the thing down to bare bones. The only way we can go cheaper is to stint on the quality of the parts, and Sanders will never go for that." Her gaze drifted up, catching mine as I hastily glanced away. "I swear I'm so tired, if there was a solution, I wouldn't see it now."

I cleared my throat then swallowed because my mouth was dry. Could she see the heat climbing up my neck? "Maybe we should call it a night. Start again when we're fresh in the morning. Our meeting's not until four."

"Sure," she murmured. Debra stood and stretched her arms over her head. The button that hadn't been able to make up its mind whether it was in or out, popped free. Her blouse parted, revealing another three inches of creamy skin and the lacy center of her ecru bra. The wire molded her curves into perfect creamy globes.

"Which bed do you want?" she asked, strolling toward the bathroom.

"Doesn't matter to me," I mumbled.

"I'll take the one closest to the AC. I'm really hot."

With that, she closed the bathroom door. I should have felt relief, but the sound of water splashing against the shower stall only heightened my arousal.

Which was crazy. I craved dick like my dachshund craved a chew toy. And why Debra? Sure her breasts were lush, but the rest of the package was a little… mismatched.

She was short, with a round face and close-cropped platinum curls nestled close to her skull. Kohl-rimmed her eyes might have made another woman look mysterious, but only made Debra seem younger. Her features were cute—snub nose, round chin, startling blue eyes—but nothing that would draw a man's *or* woman's gaze for long. Her body, however, was all grown up—lush full bosom, round hips.

In comparison, I looked like a lanky beanpole, not too tall, but together we made a very disparate pair. I'd seen the way the Advantage team had sized us up when we entered the conference room that morning, but while we looked mismatched, we'd worked together like a well-oiled machine, taking their concerns and offering options to revise the proposal that we'd present again the next day.

The door creaked open and Debra strode out, wearing only a towel and a crooked smile on her gamine face. "Forgot my pajamas."

What she pulled from the drawer beneath the television wasn't as cozy looking as she'd made it sound. A teal silk scrap spilled over her hand and she walked happily back to the bathroom.

I took the bed she didn't want and sat on the edge. Then I lay back, staring at the blades of the ceiling fan as they slowly turned again and again. Nope, the cool air didn't work. Neither did the monotonous motion.

The water stopped and Debra hummed off-key, the sound resonating through the door. I wondered if she realized she was tone deaf and couldn't help the smile that kicked up one side of my mouth.

When the door opened, she caught me smiling like an idiot. "It's all yours."

I gathered my cotton pajamas and headed to the stall. The bathroom smelled of herbal shampoo and a fruity perfume. I stripped and stepped into the stall, then turned on the faucet, not caring if the water was cool or warm. I ducked my head beneath the spray and relaxed. My attraction was transitory. Once I hit the sheets, sleep would consume my lust.

Feeling a mild disappointment that I'd so easily given up my fantasy, I opened my eyes and finished washing, taking care to shave away the bristles on my legs and pussy. So what if no one would know I'd been diligent in my hygiene. I was only stalling the moment I'd have to reenter the bedroom. I hoped like hell she was already in bed, covers pulled up to her neck, because I didn't think I could take another round of peep show without salivating.

My pajamas were decidedly unglamourous—a white tank and men's pajama bottoms. But they covered the essentials, and maybe she'd never know I was interested.

The lights were out when I opened the door. I closed it behind me, plunging myself into darkness, and felt my way toward my bed.

A light clicked on. "No need to stub a toe," Debra said.

The golden lamplight made her skin glow, and again, I couldn't help but notice her full breasts now rounding out the bodice of her short silk nightgown.

"Thanks," I said, a little too curtly. I was all out of polite. She had me rattled, starved for sex. How many weeks had it been since I'd hit Ben's apartment for a quickie?

Debra lay on her side, a hand cupping the breast pressed to the mattress. Did she know she fondled herself? Or was she making fun of me because I'd been staring?

"You know, I asked to be partnered with you," she said softly.

"Because I've worked with Advantage before?"

"Because I thought we'd have fun," she said, staring with her blue cat's eyes.

I blinked and sat on the edge of my bed. Then I reached for the light switch, but she cut my action short when she slipped the edge of her teal nightgown beneath one breast, exposing it fully. "You've been staring at it so much tonight, I thought I'd satisfy your curiosity."

Her voice held no derision or disgust. Her smile deepened, a dimple sinking into one cheek.

The breast that spilled out and lay on the white sheet was full, round, topped with a small pink nipple that was dimpled; the tip beaded like a small, dusky pebble.

"It's okay for you to touch."

Moisture flooded my pussy and my mouth. I knew I didn't want to only touch her with my fingers. I wanted to suckle that pink pearl.

"I have a boyfriend," she said, in her soft, girlish voice. At work, it annoyed me, that girly tone, but right now, it raised every hair on my arms and neck.

I pried my tongue from the roof of my mouth. "I've met him. Seems nice."

"He won't mind, Stacey."

"Mind what?" I asked stupidly, lifting my gaze from her nipple to her amazing eyes.

"If you kiss it."

No, she did not just say that! Again, I locked on her face, looking to see whether she was serious. Her smile deepened and she rolled to her back, the boob framed by the taut silk.

"It's nice...your breast...but not my thing."

"Still, you're curious," she said, her face turned toward mine. "I could tell. Your cheeks flushed every time I popped a button."

"I didn't know if you knew and didn't want to embarrass you by mentioning it."

Debra's lips parted, her white teeth flashed, and she sat up, swinging her legs over the edge of the bed. "I get it. You don't like to make the first move."

I braced my hands behind me as she approached, but her eyes narrowed, and her chin locked—a look that spelled trouble, because I'd seen it once before, when Kenneth Adams said she didn't have the right stuff to make partner.

She lifted one foot and nudged the inside of one my ankles, pushing it outward, then bent and clasped my opened knees. Her breast hovered right in front of my mouth.

"You know you want to," she whispered, then arched her back and pushed the nipple against my lips.

I opened my mouth to deny it, but she pressed inside.

My tongue pushed back, but lingered on the soft suede of her areola. The small dimples excited my tongue, and I swirled over them. The hard tip popped like those naughty buttons, elongating against the swab of my tongue until I couldn't help the urge to suck it like a straw.

Her rattling moan echoed mine, and I was too far into this thing now to pretend I didn't really want it. I reached up to cup the soft, lush breast and feed it into my mouth.

She pushed me on my back and straddled my thighs at the edge of the bed, her breast still locked between my lips.

Her body undulated, her pussy rubbing my lower belly until the motions and the heat radiating off her skin became too much, and I had to touch the rest of her, wanted to let my tongue search out other soft and sweetly responsive parts of her body.

I bit her nipple and shook my head free from under her. "Too many clothes," I whispered.

She sat up, and I watched, still trapped between her legs, as she pulled off the nightgown and tossed it away. Her skin was pale, her muff several shades darker than the pale blonde hair framing her tense face. She climbed off me and lay on her back.

I sat up immediately, shimmied out of my tank and bottoms and climbed between her spread legs, not stopping until my torso completely covered hers. "Your boyfriend's pretty open-minded."

"He wants to hear all about it. Will you mind if I tell him?"

"You planned this?"

Her smile was pure Cheshire Cat. "He likes to watch, too."

"Ever do this with a guy...while he watched?"

"Now, that *would* be cheating."

I grunted softly at the hint of mischief in her words. "Does he do it with a guy while *you* watch?"

An eyebrow arched. "My, you do have a dirty mind."

"Just curious." The talk was making me more comfortable—enough to really begin enjoying the heat of soft skin and pillowy curves beneath me.

Her eyes narrowed, the outer corners canting higher. "I've watched you. You're quiet, but those big brown eyes of yours don't miss a thing."

"That why you always manage to drop something next to my desk?"

"I like you to know what color panties I'm wearing, and you've never complained."

"Maybe I was just being polite."

"Or maybe you were trying to see if I was wet."

I pressed my lips together, then gave her the smile she'd worked so hard to coax from me. "You were."

Her eyes widened innocently. "And here I thought you'd never given this a single thought."

I didn't answer. I hadn't thought about this...exactly, but I'd wanted to know what she looked like naked for a long, long time. I stared down at the breast I kneaded with my hand, and pinched her nipple hard.

Her head tilted back, digging into the mattress, and she gasped hard. "Nice," she groaned. "All over the awkward part, I see."

Again, I huffed a breath, wondering how she read me so well.

We didn't know each other, not really, but I did feel more confident. I was ready to give this a try. I scooted down her body, suctioning and biting at her skin, watching her belly jump as I neared her sex.

I paused at her belly button and fucked it with my tongue, swirling inside and pushing against the center as though pressing an ignition button.

And she did catch fire. She gripped my head and pushed me down.

I'd never tasted another woman's pussy, only my own on my fingers or a lover's lips. Still, I knew how I liked to be touched. I thumbed apart her lips and slid my tongue along her slit, breathing in her pungent, musky aroma and capturing her salty, creamy flavor.

Her pussy tightened; liquid spilled onto my tongue. Her fingers clawed at my hair, trying to pull me up, but I didn't want to abandon my exploration.

"Give me yours," she pleaded.

That I would do. I crawled like a crab, circling my ass around, then spread my knees and lowered my pussy to her face.

Her hands guided me into place, and her lips latched onto my folds and suckled.

Her knees came up. Her hips undulated, a silent plea for me to deepen my search. I pulsed above her head and sighed when fingers stroked my cunt.

Following her lead, I leaned my weight on one elbow, thumbed her clit and tucked my fingers, three of them, inside her. Her lips and entrance clasped and relaxed, over and over, milking my digits. I thrust them deeper and bent to rub my lips over the knot at the top of her sex, peeking from beneath the thin hood. The more I rubbed, the more the hood retracted, exposing her clit. I latched my lips around it and suckled, forgetting the fingers

thrusting inside me, the mouth gobbling at my clit, and concentrated on sucking the knot until the rounded head poked out far
enough I could work my lips around it. I sucked the mini-cock,
flicking it with the point of my tongue inside my mouth, then
roughing over the whole bulb with the flat of my tongue while
her body quaked and quivered beneath mine.

Her mouth fell away from me. Her hands wrapped around
my ass and her body curled, pumping up her hips. Then she
shouted, the sound muffled against my inner thigh, and I let
go of her clit and withdrew my fingers, calming her with long
strokes of my tongue.

I rolled away and sat up, staring at her.

Her hair was spiked, her face wet with my excitement. I bent
and sucked her lips, taking the taste of me away when I leaned
back.

Her eyes blinked and her smile, this time less confident, tilted
the corners of her swollen lips. "Wow."

I grinned. "Fast learner, I guess."

"You didn't…"

"No, but I kinda like being on the bottom when I come."

"Give me a minute." Her hand glided along my arm and then
she pulled me, bringing me down beside her. We lay facing each
other. Her hands stroked my breasts, squeezed my nipples, then
slid over the curve of my hip.

Her jagged breathing quieted and the suspense flared hotter
as I wondered whether she'd follow through or want to sleep.
I was okay either way. My body was boneless, even without an
enervating orgasm. I felt as if I'd climbed a mountain or run a
long race—triumphant, self-confident, competent.

At last, Debra pushed me on my back. She snagged a pillow
from the top of the bed. "Lift up your ass."

I let her slide it under me, let her arrange my thighs wide apart, hissed when she traced my slit with her fingertips. I took a deep breath and lowered my head to the mattress. I had the feeling I wouldn't want to waste the energy to hold it up and watch.

"I bet you like to be fucked hard," she said, starchy humor back in her little-girl voice.

I grunted because she thrust all her fingers inside me and was twisting her hand while her thumb rasped over my clit.

My pussy ached, my entrance stretched. I hadn't had a big dick in a long time, and her small hand, even curved to fit, was too much.

"Do you like dick? I mean, do you eat it, rub your face on it?"

"Yessss," I hissed, my hips jerking because she'd crammed impossibly deeper.

"I love to slurp, make a lot of noise. Would you care if I got messy?"

She didn't wait for an answer, she pulled her hand free and dropped her face between my legs and rolled it in my pussy. When she looked up, her face was wet, streaks of cream clinging to her eyelashes, her cheeks.

Her smile was devilish and I returned it. She crawled up my body and kissed my mouth, and I tasted myself and licked at the cream as she closed her eyes and let me clean her up.

Our breasts were pressed together, her nipples spiking against mine, and she looked down at our chests. "I'll fuck you. Then I want to come back to suck a while. Will you like that?"

I nodded, beyond words because my body was hot and tense, my pussy drowning.

She edged off the mattress and padded to the same drawer where she'd pulled out the nightgown and lifted a dildo for me to see.

I wasn't sure if I was happy or disappointed. I'd liked the

personal attention, liked her face between my legs, her soft eyelashes grazing my clit, her nose and mouth rubbing in my juices.

She flicked a switch at the base and sauntered toward the bed. I lifted my knees higher and splayed my thighs. Now I wanted to watch, so I grabbed the second pillow to shove beneath my head.

Debra teased my entrance with the gel head, rimming it, just a hint of vibration, but enough to get my pussy sucking.

She pulled the dildo away again and bent to kiss my clit and tongue my pussy lips. "You shave, not a single bristle. *Mmmm.*"

The tip of the dildo dipped inside again, but swirled only once, then trailed downward toward my ass.

Her cat's eyes glanced up to catch my gaze. "Yeah, didn't think I'd use it on your cunt, did you?" She used her thumb and finger to open my tiny entrance, then leaned closer and spat. The dildo swirled over my asshole and twisted around and around, then pushed inside.

I'd enjoyed anal play with a boyfriend once, so the dildo didn't shock me. But the vibrations made it different, made it new. She worked it inside in slow, sure strokes then turned up the speed.

I was sweating now, my pussy spasming, clasping air. She knelt between my legs and thrust the plastic cock with one hand and used her tongue and teeth to coax my arousal higher.

My whole body shivered, my legs trembled. I cupped my breasts and rubbed them while she stroked her tongue over my lips and fucked my ass. When her mouth latched on to my clit and sucked, I came—so hard my eyes squeezed shut and my breath caught. Everywhere she stroked and licked and bit was too hard, too much—and absolutely perfect.

She eased me down with gentle kisses and long swipes of her tongue over the length of my pussy. The dildo left, leaving my ass a little sore but pulsing along with the waning convulsions that rippled up my vagina.

Debra kissed my belly then came up my body, resting her head between my breasts. "I knew we'd be good."

My hands petted her spiky hair. My thighs cupped the sides of hers. We lay shaken and gasping. I wished we had another day and night to stay inside this room and explore this...thing... we had.

"You know, we should set an early alarm."

"Yeah, work." I mumbled, not able to deal with verbal communication just yet.

"If we get this bid, I bet Sanders will think we make a good team."

A smile tugged at my lips as I followed her train of thought.

"He'd send us on more client meet and greets. More presentations." She lifted her head and caught the edge of her bottom lip between her teeth. "That is, if you'd like to do this again."

I cradled her face between my hands. "I'll be your 'out-of-towner,' Deb."

"Whew!" She wrinkled her nose. "Thought maybe you weren't that into this."

I rolled my eyes. "You didn't hear that little scream?"

"No, you were gasping, but no moans or screams. Thought I wasn't getting it."

"I didn't have the breath to do it out loud."

She smiled wickedly, and her eyelids drooped. "Liked it that much, did you?"

"Guess you'll have to prove it wasn't a fluke."

"We really should sleep," she said, waggling her eyebrows. "Can't be yawning in front of the Advantage guys."

I couldn't help the laugh. We were anything but tired. "We'll sleep. *After.*"

Our lips suctioned together, greedily, each of us moaning into the other's mouth.

Debra lifted her head. "I think…you won't mind so much if he watches." A hand slipped between my legs; fingers entered my cunt and tunneled deep.

"He can offer suggestions," I gasped, rolling my hips to fuck the swirling digits.

"But no touching." Her lips curved, the dimple sinking deep.

I reached up and kissed the end of her snub nose. "Nope. That would be cheating."

REBEL GIRL

Kirsty Logan

He grabs a fistful of Evie's hair as he comes, pulling her close to his chest, whispering guttural curses into the side of her neck. His cock thrusts deeper into her, the ridge of the head rubbing her in just the right place, and she's so close, just one more...but he's already growing soft inside her, the condom puckered and wet.

She rolls off him, starts digging through her skirt pocket for her lighter and tobacco. He's wriggling back into his clothes, all elbows and legs in the cramped backseat. Evie rolls her cigarette expertly, fingers twisting and tightening like a magic trick as she looks out of the sweat-blurred windows at the car parked next to theirs. She hopes Katia is having more success with her man.

She can see vague shapes, knees raised and palms pressing out for balance. She imagines Katia, head thrust back and tits pushed out, sliding her slick cunt up and down on the endlessly hard cock. She tells herself she's only thinking these things because she's jealous, because Katia gets to ride her way to an explosive orgasm and Evie does not.

* * *

Katia has a mouth on her nipple and a cock in her cunt and she's moaning, "Oh, yes, oh, fuck, oh, yes." She's so close, almost cresting the wave, almost crowning the hill, and she feels the blood drain from her brain to her clit. He comes, grunting an approximation of her name, and collapses with his head on her chest. She squirms under him, trying for release, but he's wrinkling away to nothing and the feeling has gone.

The backseat is sticky with sex and sweat. Katia feels around on the floor for her bra, wishing he'd wake up and get off her so she can get some air. The summer is humid, so hot she sweats in a bra and shorts, her skin always reddened and slightly swollen from the heat. Over the top of his head, the sweat-dampened curls behind his ear, she can see the car parked beside theirs. The windows are opaque with smoke, and it's stopped juddering on its chassis. Katia imagines Evie, sated and soaking into the leather fabric of the backseat, a slow smile on her face. Katia is sure Evie just had the best orgasm of her life; she is sure every single one of Evie's orgasms is the best of her life.

All four of them are sprawled on the hoods of the cars—boys on one, girls on the other. They listen to the lullaby of the motorway and stare up at the dirty orange sky. The night air smells hot and dense. Beneath a low moon, the town cowers: smokestacks, parking lots, roundabouts. Everything has washed out to gray. Katia and Evie share a cigarette, ringing the filter with sticky lip-gloss in varying shades of pink.

Katia smokes like she's sucking a cock, slow and deliberate, a performance. She knows Evie is watching her, and she arches her body slightly on the hood so Evie can see the curve of her back-hips-tits. Katia knows Evie has a crush on her because she's older and always has a boyfriend. Katia has a crush on Evie too, because she has high round tits and a rosebud mouth and makes amazing noises when she fucks. Evie likes Katia because she is jaded, and Katia likes Evie because she is not.

The boys are still looking up at the sky, but they start to make grumbling noises. They want cigarettes, beer, music. They start jingling the car keys in their pockets, but the road down the hill is pitted and neither car's suspension makes any difference.

Without conferring, the girls slide off the hood, their skirts riding up and flashing their brightly colored thongs. Hand in hand, they walk down the winding hill toward the beacon of the all-night garage.

Wearing sunglasses inside at night makes Evie feel like a movie star. They aren't just a conceit: the fluorescents inside the garage are blinding after the dim glow of the car's interior light. Evie's calves are itching and gray from the dusty path, her skirt stuck to her thighs with sweat. The garage's air-conditioning is cold enough to make her nipples harden, and she crosses her arms over her chest so the guy behind the counter can't see. She paws through the meager collection of wares. Tree-shaped air fresheners, trees on the labels of the mineral water, *Country Life* magazines full of trees. It's fucking stupid: nothing around here even resembles a tree.

Katia snorts, and Evie looks up. Katia is standing, arms akimbo, face raised to the top shelf of the magazine rack. She waits for Evie to walk over then grabs an armful of the magazines. Evie looks over Katia's shoulder at the plastic-wrapped covers showing girls with glazed eyes and black bars over their nipples. She's close enough to smell Katia's hair: sweet fruity shampoo under bitter hairspray. Katia pulls one of the magazines out of the plastic bag and flips through it. Every page is a different girl, her hair dyed and legs spread. There are no black bars on the inside pages, and the girls' cunts are spread open, the bull's-eye of every image.

Evie's clit throbs. The images aren't sexy, but she can't stop staring at the honesty of their open legs. Their tits are clearly fake, high on their ribs and beach ball–tight. But their cunts are pure truth: wet and pink, like steak freshly cut. Evie wonders whether Katia's clit is throbbing too.

Katia is pretty sure she knows more about Evie's sexual tastes from those blurry glimpses through the car window than her own boyfriend. Although Evie is acting like she's totally unfazed by the array of cunts, Katia knows otherwise. She can tell by the way Evie is shifting her weight from one leg to the other, the way she's chewing on her lip, the loudening of her breath. When Evie walked over to the magazine rack, Katia could see her nipples through the thin fabric of her bikini top. Katia knows that Evie can probably see her nipples too, but she doesn't give a shit. She doesn't even care if the perv behind the counter can see. Katia has great tits, and she knows it, and so the whole fucking world can stare.

Katia jams the magazines back onto the top shelf and turns to Evie. She looks stoned, pupils huge and mouth hanging slack. Katia pulls Evie's chin, opening her mouth farther, imagining it will snap back and start rolling up window blind–style like in a cartoon. It's meant to be a joke, but standing there with her heat-swollen hands on Evie's jaw she can see the tiny lines of her lip, can feel the stickiness of her lip-gloss on the tip of her thumb, and it doesn't feel very funny. Katia is suddenly aware of the buzzing fluorescents, the dust itching her legs, the slow stare of the man behind the counter. Her clit feels swollen, her nipples tight. All the pressure in the air seems to coalesce between her legs.

She knows what she should do: let go of Evie, buy cigarettes for the boys, go back out into the dusty night and climb the hill back to that sweaty backseat. She takes Evie's hand and leads her out the back door of the garage.

Walking outside feels like crawling under a blanket. The air is hot and completely still, and Evie can feel the sweat already prickling on the small of her back. She hopes her palms won't feel wet against Katia's. Her whole body feels tight, her skin as thin as an expanding balloon.

They forgot to buy the cigarettes, and Evie is about to mention it when Katia spins her around and presses her up against the brick wall of the garage and slides her tongue into Evie's mouth. All the blood rushes out of Evie's head. She kisses Katia back just to stay standing. The atmosphere is so humid she can barely take a breath, the air like cotton wool in her lungs.

Katia kisses hard, but her lips are soft and she tucks Evie's hair behind her ear before pulling away to smile at her. Evie has Katia's tits pressed up against her tits, Katia's legs tangled in her legs, Katia's fingers entwined with her fingers. All she can think to do is return the smile. Katia seems to take this as consent. She lifts Evie's hair in her hands, piling it up and pressing her palms against the heat of Evie's neck, before kissing her again.

Katia has two heartbeats, one in her chest and one between her legs, and she's pressed up so close to Evie that she must be able to feel both. Evie's skin smells sweet and metallic: fresh perspiration and sugary lip-gloss and boys. Evie's body feels unfamiliar pressed against her own, with bumps where boys don't have them and an absence where they usually do. Katia wonders how she is supposed to know if Evie wants to fuck—she's used to the reassurance of a hard cock against her hip. She stops for a moment, unsure, and Evie wriggles against her, pressing her pelvic bone against Katia's, and then she knows for sure that Evie wants to fuck.

Evie loves having her nipples sucked, and judging from the way Katia immediately takes them into her mouth, she seems aware of the fact. She sucks hard, and Evie's thong is already sliding up into her slickening cunt, the fabric uncomfortable against her swollen clit. Evie's skirt is up around her hips, her bikini top shoved to the side, and she pushes her thong down with one hand and guides Katia's fingers into her with the other.

Katia slides two fingers in, curling them round so the pads press against that little patch of ridged skin, the web between finger and thumb pressing against Evie's clit. Evie can't make words so she just rolls her eyes up to the fading sky and rides Katia's fingers, feeling her wetness pool in Katia's palm. Katia presses her up against the gritty brick wall, fucking her harder, and then Evie feels it, the crest of the wave, the tip of the mountain, and the feeling throbs from her clit to her throat and back down again to settle low in her belly. She can feel her cunt spasming around Katia's fingers, and before the feeling fades she drops to her knees and pulls Katia's thong to the side.

Katia's cunt tastes like wet dirt and salt, and it doesn't matter that Evie doesn't know what she's supposed to do because as soon as she finds that little knot of flesh she hooks on to it, sucking it into her mouth, and Katia is grabbing the back of her head and grinding against her chin and she can feel Katia's cunt spasming against her tongue. The girls stagger to their feet, eyes blurred and knees unsteady. They rearrange their clothes without looking, awkward around each other's nakedness, and walk away from the garage.

As they reach the bottom of the hill, the first drops of a summer storm land on their shoulders. It's cool against their heat-swollen skin, slicking their hair against their heads; droplets slide down their backs. They raise their faces to the sky. The crackle of heat fades and the smell of earth rises up around them. By the time they get back to their men, the rain has washed them clean.

THE BEST KIND
OF REVENGE

Geneva King

Jana's apartment complex was too well constructed.

It was late Thursday and the only work request had come from Mrs. Jenkins. The old girl had to be pushing ninety and Jana had no interest in exploring her drawers.

Instead, she'd been put to work cleaning gutters and sweeping the walkways, watching the tenants as they went about their lives.

4D: White lacy panties with matching bras. Box of condoms in the nightstand beside the bed. Never went anywhere without her husband and didn't speak unless someone specifically asked her a question.

3F: Dressed in plain suits with ugly black flats. Jana had been pleasantly surprised by her collection of colorful thongs.

1B lived alone. Didn't speak much but kept a small dildo nestled underneath her pillow. Its velvety head felt realistic. She loved the way it felt as she squeezed her hand around it, imagining her fingers were 1B's pelvic muscles as she approached climax. Even the sharp latex hadn't been able to mask 1B's scent. She'd run her tongue over the toy trying to get a taste of the mysterious woman.

Jana wasn't a pervert. She loved women, loved women's things, loved discovering her tenants' secrets. It gave her a rush to learn something about each of them. So far, she'd gotten away with it. Most people never paid much attention to the help. She was almost invisible.

The process was simple. When she'd get a call, she'd help herself to a peek in their bedrooms. It had become her private little game, trying to guess what the tenants wore under their clothes, who was kinky, who wasn't.

Jana jabbed the ground viciously. It'd been over a week with no broken dishwashers or blown lights. The drains didn't even have the decency to clog.

She perked up when the tenant in 2C walked past her to the front office.

"They're out to lunch," Jana called. "Can I help you with something?"

2C pursed her lips, annoyance flashing across her pretty features. "I need to pay rent. I don't think I'll be back until late."

"I'll take it for you." Jana dropped the broom and led her inside. "If you give me a second, I'll write you a receipt."

"Thanks." 2C sat on the couch.

Jana bent over the counter, taking care not to be too obvious as she studied the tenant. Her light pink toenails were encased in expensive-looking strappy heels. 2C shifted in her seat, revealing the top of her thigh-high stockings, held in place by the strap of a garter belt.

Jana clenched her legs tight as a familiar lust coursed through her body. She prayed she wouldn't embarrass herself.

"Is everything all right with the apartment?" She tore the receipt carefully, trying to prolong the visit. Maybe she'd get lucky and 2C's skirt would fly up.

2C nodded briskly. "Everything is fine." She paused. "Except for one thing. I think the smoke detector needs a new battery. Is that my job or..."

Jackpot. Jana directed a prayer toward heaven as she started a work ticket. "I'll be glad to take care of that for you."

2C smiled for the first time. "Thanks. That beeping sound was driving me insane." With a look at her watch, she took the rent receipt from Jana and left the office.

Jana waited until 2C drove off the property before going up to the apartment. Her fingers trembled even as she tried to control herself. The last thing she needed was to be busted on suspicion of theft. After several attempts, she managed to get the key in the lock and stepped inside.

2C was still in the midst of unpacking. Boxes lined the living room walls. Jana took a cursory peek in one: office supplies. Boring.

The bedroom was much neater. Jana sidled inside and prepared to go to work.

Most women stored their underwear in the top dresser drawer. Bingo. Last year's Victoria's Secret collection spilled into her hands. She picked up one, bright red, and buried her face in the fabric. They smelled nice, like springtime rain, but that wasn't the fragrance she was after.

Rule number one: leave everything exactly as you found it. She fixed the drawers before moving on to find the laundry hamper. Jana dug around until she found a black pair of underwear. 2C's pungent scent filled her nose; her own panties grew damp as her body stirred with hunger. With an effort, she pulled herself together. This was not the time or place for release.

Last on the list was the nightstand. Nothing. Her gaze fell on a small trunk sticking out from under the bed. Jana tried to open it. Locked. She eyed the latch, imagining what treasures were hidden inside. She had to have some kind of tool that would fit.

BEEP!

Jana dropped the chest and shot off the bed, afraid 2C had come home early.

Then she recognized the sound of the smoke alarm. In her excitement, she'd almost forgotten about it. *Rule number two*: don't leave without getting the job done. She glanced back at the trunk but was too shaken to investigate further. She pushed it back under the bed and took a last reluctant sniff of the panties before returning them to the hamper.

That night, Jana stayed in her apartment and pulled out her prized video collection, eager to relive her trip to 2C.

Just as the bored housewife stripped for the well-muscled mail woman, her cell phone rang. She looked at the screen and sighed, irritated. Marge always interrupted at the wrong moment.

Her boss's sleepy voice filled the phone. "Jana, can you go to 2C? She's got some kind of emergency leak. Just do what you can for tonight."

"Sure." Jana climbed out of bed and pulled on her jeans. Her trips were never any fun when the tenant was actually there, but maybe she'd find some clues about where to search next time.

2C opened the door in a see-through nightgown. Jana momentarily lost her ability to speak at the sight of the large nipples caressing the fabric.

She swallowed. "Marge said you've got a leak?" Even as she asked, a seed of doubt unfurled in her mind. 2C looked too put together and, above all, too dry to have been fighting a leak.

Before she could move, 2C pulled her into the apartment. "Yes, follow me. It's in my bathroom."

Jana was following her down the hall, not even bothering to keep her eyes off the rounded hips swaying in front of her, when suddenly someone grabbed her arm and pulled her aside.

Jana cried out; a strange hand instantly covered her mouth. The room was too dark to make out her attacker—or attackers. She felt more than two hands grabbing her. She struggled but they quickly overpowered and pinned her to the floor.

Her eyes flooded with light. She blinked. Her captors stood, staring at her, grim expressions on their faces. The ladies from 4D, 3F and 1B were all similarly clad in lingerie. Jana's stomach dropped. When she dreamed of this, there were smiles. This looked like something out of a Stephen King movie.

Still, she feigned innocence. "What's going on? Where's the flood?"

2C reappeared, holding the box. "I see you found my little trunk."

Jana shook her head, but 2C silenced her with a look. "Don't lie to me, Jana. I know you tried to open it."

"Just like you opened our drawers," 4D added.

"We have to admit, you were good. You were very careful."

"We almost didn't realize it, but when she mentioned the trunk, we put two and two together."

Tears welled in Jana's eyes, almost constricting her throat. "Are you going to report me?"

The women looked at one another. Finally, 3F spoke. "We were, but then we realized it wouldn't solve anything."

"It's not like you stole from us." 4D shot Jana a steely glare. "You didn't, did you?"

"No, never!"

It had never been about taking things, even when the desire for a keepsake was strong. Jana shrank under their gazes. It occurred to her that of all the women, 4D's presence was the most surprising. Jana had never seen her without her husband and she didn't seem like the forceful type.

"We didn't think so. However, we can't allow you to go unpunished."

Their eyes became more wolflike as they crowded around her, until all she could see was the lace of their outfits. And legs. Long, smooth, curvy legs. Jana sighed, momentarily forgetting her precarious situation.

"You're gonna have your way with me?" She tried not to sound too hopeful.

"Don't get cute," 1B snapped. She turned to 2C. "Tell her what she's won."

2C snapped open her trunk and withdrew a wooden hairbrush. "For your crimes, Jana, you will receive a sound thrashing." She smacked the brush against her palm.

"Bare-assed."

"Definitely."

The terror of losing her job turned into fear of her impending sentence. And still deep down, the thought of these four formerly docile women dominating her seemed more exciting than threatening.

Jana nodded slowly. "As you wish."

They released her. "Stand up. Strip."

Jana did as ordered, hesitantly handing her jeans and T-shirt to 1B. 3F placed a chair in the middle of the room and sat. "Over my knee."

For the first time she noticed the other chairs in the room. The others pulled them out in a semicircle around 3F. They sat, legs crossed, and watched her expectantly. Jana hesitantly draped her body over 3F's legs and squeezed her eyes shut.

"The brush," 2C said pleasantly. Too pleasantly.

"Thank you, dear." 3F sounded as if she were taking biscuits from the queen, not preparing to paddle Jana's hide until it was raw.

Bristles ran over Jana's backside. Her body tensed in both anticipation and anxiety over what she felt certain was going to be a rough paddling.

She was right. The hard back of the brush hit her flesh and she cried out.

"Not a peep from you or you'll get more."

3F grunted from the exertion but never paused. There was no rhythm, no cadence that Jana could discern, no way to anticipate the next one. Jana clenched her fists, trying to keep her mind off the pain radiating across her ass. It didn't work; the sensation intensified until her ass screamed for relief.

2C paused. "Good job, there you go." With a jolt, Jana realized the voice came from behind her, the cool assessing eyes probably fixed on her exposed cheeks. "Who's next?"

"Me! I'll go." 4D jumped up and ran her fingers in circles over Jana's flesh.

It hurt like hell, but she wasn't going to give them the satisfaction of knowing that. She remained draped over 3F's lap, ass completely exposed to the ravenous women watching her.

"Her skin's so red."

"That's how you know she's learning a lesson." 2C sounded amused, like she was talking to a curious child. "Feel between her legs. See how much she's enjoying this."

"Bitch," Jana thought viciously, as 4D's fingers probed her pussy lips for proof of her body's betrayal.

4D sucked in a deep breath. "Ooh, you're right." Jana could only imagine 4D's wonderment at seeing another woman. She'd probably never seen herself up close and personal. She fondled Jana deep inside with one finger, then another, until Jana squirmed with the effort of keeping silent, this time quelling moans of pleasure.

Abruptly, the other woman stopped. "I'm ready."

Jana mourned the loss as the brush changed hands. She hoped 4D would be merciful.

No such luck. 4D seemed determined to beat every bit of wetness out of Jana with her erratic strokes. Where 3F concentrated on one spot, 4D left no patch of skin unpaddled. Jana covered her mouth, but a groan escaped from her lips. She froze, hoping they hadn't heard it.

"Stop." 2C's calves appeared in front of her. "Didn't we tell you to keep silent?"

"Yes," Jana mumbled.

"Yes, what?"

"Yes, ma'am," she said through clenched teeth.

She heard muffled whispers behind her and knew they were planning her punishment. More spankings? She was already supposed to get more of those—unless 2C had something worse than a hairbrush in her trunk.

That damn trunk. That's what had gotten her in this situation in the first place.

I need to masturbate, she thought, shamefully. Jana's ass was on fire, but now her clit was heavy with need, thanks to 4D's explorations; the need to feel those fingers back inside her, thrusting her into orgasm.

She knew better than to ask for release.

Someone hauled her roughly off 3F's lap. 2C's smiling face came into view. She pointed to 1B. "She doesn't want to spank you; she thinks you've had enough."

Jana looked between the women, unsure of what to do.

2C frowned. "You should thank her."

"Thank...you," Jana managed. Was this it? Was she being released? It was a relief to her throbbing behind, but yet, she felt cheated.

2C continued. "We were thinking. We're doing all this work turning you on. You are turned on, aren't you?"

Jana opened her mouth, ready to disagree, but the words didn't come. They all knew it would be a lie. "Yes," she said, finally.

"Like we thought. Then we said, this isn't fair. She should be turning us on." Her voice hardened. "Get on your knees and don't move until she's come."

"I hope you're good with your mouth," 3F said, smirking.

Jana's ass ached as she knelt on the ground. 1B spread her legs, underwear removed, pussy ready and waiting for Jana's mouth.

"Any day now." 2C pushed Jana's head into 1B's cunt.

So much for finesse, Jana thought as she went to work drawing her tongue along 1B's fat pussy lips. The woman moaned and bucked, pushing her pelvis deeper into Jana's face. She wrapped her lips around the engorged clit as 1B's juices dripped from her body.

"Oh, Jana." 1B clutched Jana's head to her body until she could barely breathe, but now, surrounded by 1B's scents and grunts, it wasn't important. Her attention was focused on pleasuring this woman the way she'd fantasized.

The others worked her exposed body, but now their fingers were a welcome intrusion: in her pussy, around her lips, up her slit and into her...anus?

She jerked up, but 1B forced her head back down. "No!"

Something cool slid down her crack as 2C spoke. "Don't move. Don't stop. Just keep going."

"But, wait!" Jana protested as the foreign object twisted

inside her. She'd never explored anal play and, besides, weren't you supposed to prepare first?

"Honestly, such fuss over a little butt plug." 2C pressed the toy until it reached the hilt. "I don't hear an orgasm."

"Almost. There." 1B gasped. Angrily, Jana went back to work, working 1B's clit until she felt 1B's legs clench and stiffen around her.

Jana extricated herself and looked down at the woman splayed beneath her. She admired her handiwork. Now that she'd had a moment to adjust, the plug didn't feel so...intrusive.

2C smiled, her ever calm voice steady as she rooted through her trunk. "There. Not so bad, is it, Jana?"

The other women laughed and Jana glared back, frustration bubbling up inside of her. This was ridiculous! Maybe she had been wrong for looking through their personal stuff. She was a big girl, she could admit when she was wrong. But this, this was insane. Being taunted and humiliated and spanked and—

2C noticed. "I think our girl needs some time to collect herself. Go to the corner, Jana."

This bitch had another thing coming, if she seriously expected Jana to sit in time-out like a child.

"Go to hell."

2C sighed. "Jana, Jana, Jana. And you were doing so well."

She pulled out a large rubber dildo and a harness. Without looking away, 2C strapped herself in with a dexterity Jana couldn't help but admire. For the first time, the others looked wary. 3F exchanged confused glances with 1B, but 4D stared in wide-eyed fascination at the scene before her.

2C sat in a chair. "Come here."

Jana didn't move. The cock was huge, too big for her. In any case, she wasn't interested in being a tool for this woman's amusement.

"You feel it, don't you? That need." Her voice was almost hypnotic. "Come on, Jana, let's release it."

Jana walked over hesitantly and straddled 2C's lap, hovering over the dildo. Her eyes locked with her nemesis, her only shot at relief, until the fat dildo head penetrated and slid inside her.

2C gripped Jana's asscheeks as she bounced and Jana cried out against the conflicting sensations: pain radiating from her tender bottom, pleasure from the cock filling her pussy.

2C lifted her, then lowered her back onto the dildo, the calmness in her eyes lessening with each movement.

"Have you learned your lesson, Jana?" 2C whispered. "This is what happens to naughty girls who stick their noses where they don't belong."

"Yes, ma'am," Jana croaked.

"Sheryl. Just Sheryl." Sheryl nipped the side of her neck tenderly.

"Yes, 2-Sheryl," Jana cried out, no longer concerned with her audience or the nature of her crimes, just caring about the orgasm crashing down around her, reverberating through her body until she was too weak to do more than slump against 2C.

2C held her as she wept, gingerly patting her back. Then all too soon, she felt soft hands lifting her up. Quickly, they helped her dress before guiding her to the door and sending her out.

Three days later, Jana fixed the lights outside the manager's office—three days of no peeping, no rifling through her tenants' things. Her still-sore bottom did a very good job of keeping her honest.

Marge walked up and tapped Jana on the shoulder. "I got a work order for you. The lady says her faucets are dripping."

Jana turned to see 2C opening her car door. She winked at Jana before slipping inside and starting the engine.

ONE EIGHTY

Carrie Cannon

Madison knew how to cook. She honed her skills at the French Laundry and used to be the chef at the hottest fine-dining restaurant in town.

Madison did her own home repairs. She didn't just caulk her own tub; she laid her own roofing and hung her own Sheetrock.

Her house was always clean.

Madison went to Smith. Madison was trilingual. Madison and her husband kayaked waterfalls in Venezuela every year.

Madison. Madison. Madison. Madison.

The four of us were supposed to be great friends—every other weekend together barbecuing, the last two summers sharing a beach house—but in the past few months Madison had crawled under my skin and started moving in furniture. It was bad enough my husband pulled out his binoculars every time she and her bouncing breasts mowed the yard in a sports bra; did she have to be so damned gracious, too?

Never angry or sullen; unflinchingly helpful; ridiculously, absurdly nice: she didn't deserve to live.

I hated her most at night. Her bedroom window faced mine. Each night she would enter her room and raise the blinds. It doesn't occur to the Beautiful People to be modest. She'd remove one article of clothing after another, until nothing remained but luminous skin, rosy nipples, and an oh-so-neatly trimmed triangle of pubic hair. Then she'd languorously drop a thin silken shift over her head and let it shimmy down to drape her slim body.

Sometimes she'd lean against the window with the light from her bedroom shining through her gossamer gown and defining every nuance of her silhouette. I'd stay hidden in the shadowy darkness of my room, secretly watching as she was lost in her private, perfect world, unaware of the mere mortal glaring daggers at her twenty feet away. Every night this oblivious act of exhibitionism left me seething with a nameless rage, sweating and tossing in my bed, until late in the night.

I couldn't stand her. I couldn't stop thinking about her. I spent afternoons imagining it was Madison's size-four ass I was grinding up in the disposal with the Cheerios and Pop-Tart remains from breakfast. *That's right, I don't get around to cleaning up breakfast until just before dinner; what's my punishment for that crime, Madison?* It felt like a phantom Madison was watching me from every window and every dark corner of my house, secretly observing, summing me up, finding me lacking in a way the real Madison, the Pollyanna-perfect Madison never would be.

One afternoon when Ellie and Jack were at school and Blake was at work, I shoved piles of laundry aside and lay back on the couch to reread my favorite chapter in *Wuthering Heights*. I slid one hand down the front of my pajama pants, ready to take a beating from Heathcliff, but his throbbing gypsy erection had no chance with Madison hovering, watching and judging, distracting me with her immaculate perfection. Just to show her, I grunted even louder and came even harder, skin burning beneath the self-righteous glare of those imaginary eyes.

When Madison told us she was going to start volunteering at the Children's Hospital, it was the last straw.

"I want to sell the house," I told Blake. "Let's move to Tucson."

"What the hell are you talking about? You love this house."

"I need a change."

"What's gotten into you? I can't switch my job to Tucson; the kids are happy here. You're just in another one of your moods."

"What's the matter, afraid Miss Cuppa at the coffee shop would miss you?"

"Drop it, all right? If you need a change why don't you finally paint the other half of the living room or do something with that snaky pile of boards in the backyard you keep referring to as 'the deck?'"

The next morning I proudly showed him the sleek, polished-nickel faucet that absolutely had to go in the kitchen. Madison wasn't the only one who could do things.

"You're going to replace plumbing?" He blanched.

"What's your point?" I asked, eyes narrowing. He snapped his jaw shut and left without another comment.

Five hours later I had screamed myself hoarse. I had gnashed my teeth and torn my hair. I had collapsed in a dejected puddle on the floor. So what if my modern, sexy faucet had pliers gashes around the base? So what if it tilted at an odd angle? So what if there were a few extra parts lying around unaccounted for on the floor? The real problem was the house-rattling clank that ensued every time I turned the water back on. And the hissing jets that shot out from the faucet at all angles.

I cursed the faucet, cursed my rotten home-improvement skills, and cursed Madison for good measure. Then I slumped against the counter and resolved to throw myself at a plumber. He could take anything he wanted if he'd just get the whole mess cleared away before Blake came home.

The doorbell rang.

I opened the door and there stood Madison. The house thumped and hissed behind me. Of course it was Madison. Madison who never comes over unannounced, Madison who just can't leave me the hell alone even though we haven't spoken in a week, Madison who was the last possible person I wanted to see at this exact moment. But those comedian Fates (who've always had it in for me) had aligned; the star charts had been written; and Mr. Murphy'd had his say. There was no way Madison could *not* darken my door at the moment of my deepest shame. Madison with…a bottle of wine? And wearing that tight little shirt that shows off her cleavage? At one o'clock?

"I heard you yelling. Is everything okay?"

Thirty minutes later the whole nightmare was history: faucet straight; pipes tamed; water whispering, calm and obsequious from the tap.

"See?" she said. "The gashes are all hidden now. All you have to do is turn this cap one eighty and everything looks pretty and shiny." I nodded as if I knew what the hell she was talking about. Part of me still hated her, but I was so damned grateful I couldn't do anything but grin at her like an idiot.

She just saved me from mortifying myself with the plumber, I thought. *The least I can do is drink her wine. Why on earth would she bring wine with her anyway?* As I set a glass down next to where she perched, legs crossed on top of the kitchen counter, she moved her hand to rest it lightly on top of mine. This unexpected intimacy should have surprised me, I suppose, but what surprised me was the thrill of electricity that ran up my arm. I found myself strangely aware of the curve of her neck, the rounded protrusion of her collarbone, those flawless orbs on her chest that were barely contained behind straining fabric. I shook my head to clear the fog hijacking my concentration.

"Madison? Why did you bring a bottle of wine with you?"

She turned crimson. "You know, I've always really admired you, Susan. Truth is, I've always been a little jealous of you."

That was carrying things too far. And what did any of this have to do with that bottle of wine? I gently extracted my hand. With a surge of something almost like regret, I moved across the kitchen and leaned against the counter. "Oh, please," I said. "You can do anything."

"I can't be fearless like you are. You're wonderfully intense and you're never ashamed to say what you think. You're not even afraid to tell off that scary bitch who runs the neighborhood association." She shook her head. "No, I could never do that."

I blushed. That had been a proud moment for me. "That old bag?" I answered modestly. "What's so scary about her?"

Her eyes caught mine and the faintest hint of pink remained on her cheeks. I felt my own cheeks go hot again. I couldn't stop staring at the outline of her pale lips. "I've always been jealous of your relationship with Blake, too," the lips said.

I choked on my wine. "What? I mean, why?" There was something coy about the way she put the emphasis on 'Blake,' as though she were jealous of him, not the relationship.

"The way he looks at you—he must think about fucking you all the time." The look in her eyes made me wonder suddenly if she'd thought about it once or twice herself, and my stomach got all twisty and excited. Was Madison coming on to me? Did I want her to? Wasn't I poking sewing needles into a canvas Madison doll just this morning?

I snorted in response. "Blake thinks about fucking everything all the time. Blake would figure out how to fuck a porcupine if it sat still long enough. Mark doesn't like to have sex?"

"Oh, it's not that; he's...enthusiastic." The word fell between us like a lead weight. "Don't get me wrong; I love him. He's just not terribly..."

"Terribly what?" My eyes were wide. I was having trouble catching my breath and my head was getting fuzzy again. The air between us snapped and crackled with tension.

"He's just...he's just not all that good. It's been years since I had an orgasm with him in the room. Oh, god, I can't believe I said it!" She burst into hysterical, nervous laughter, rolling her perfect buttcheeks back and forth across my counter. The sight of her happily jiggling breasts made my stomach do flip-flops.

She calmed herself and began intently picking breakfast crumbs off the counter, pinching and rolling them between the tips of her long, slender fingers. She fixed me with a soul-jolting stare. "Do you ever feel like you need a change?" she asked, barely above a whisper. She looked terrified.

"You mean like having a go at Gladiator Glenn, the UPS delivery guy?" I blurted, my voice cracking. I hoped that wasn't at all what she meant.

"No. Something a little more...close to home." Neither of us had moved, but she suddenly seemed very, very close. I thought I could feel her heat, hear the hiss of her breath. And those crystal blue eyes were pinning me, squirming, to my own stretch of counter.

"I'm sorry if I'm completely out of line," she said quietly, "but I came over here today to...I mean, I just wondered...the way you've watched me at night in the window the past few months. I thought I might have a chance."

I'm pretty sure I turned the same color as the pinot noir trembling in my hand. I didn't need to mortify myself with the plumber; I was doing a fine job of it right here with Madison. I guess my bedroom wasn't as dark as I thought. Then I realized this meant Madison had been undressing for me all those nights. She had known I was there…but she didn't seem to mind. And she was right, my obsession may have been couched in animosity, but it was starting to look a lot like a playground crush. Had I been yanking Madison's braids?

I couldn't speak. I fumbled and sputtered and tried to process this new Madison. The Madison who admired me. The Madison who was coming on to me. The Madison who suddenly made me want to throw her down on the kitchen tile and redefine ravage.

I found myself creeping uncertainly across the room toward her, but once my hands clasped her knees I completely lost my nerve. Fearless indeed. I'd never even kissed a woman.

"What if we get caught?" she asked, looking a little shocked herself.

"You mean by Blake? Are you kidding? He'd drop to his knees and sing praise and thanksgiving to any god who'd listen. Besides, he has a standing appointment at the coffee shop on Wednesdays."

She smiled and bit her lower lip in such a sweet way that my own lips just skipped over to join in. She seemed slight, insubstantial compared to the men I had kissed. I wasn't prepared for how rough and clumsy I would feel against her thin frame, but her eager response made my heart flutter and my skin tingle.

Her legs twined around my hips as my pelvis pressed into the hard edge of the counter. Was this the same Madison I was cursing an hour ago? The fog in my brain was back and I couldn't concentrate on anything except the heat in my chest, quickly gaining pace from a simmer to a boil. One wandering hand (mine or hers?) slipped over my rib cage and brushed my breast. Madison murmured some incoherent mantra in my ear and I became painfully aware of the thin layers of fabric separating her crotch from my waist. When my hand worked its way under her shirt, she cried out and her murmur solidified into words. "Please, please, please, oh, god, please. Please, please fuck me."

I stood back to face her with a jolt. Perfect, tidy little Madison had eyes glassed over with desperation. Perfect, composed little Madison was whimpering and begging me, of all people, to fuck her brains out. Suddenly, all the anger and resentment I had focused on Madison for the past few months was transformed into an equally fierce tenderness. At the same time, a wave of predatory lust surged through me and this heady cocktail of emotions shored up my confidence.

I touched my lips to her ear. "Get down off the counter and remove your clothes."

Madison did as I asked, dropping one article of clothing after another on the floor in a reenactment of all those previous nights. She stood before me, her pale eyes searching mine for approval, her pink nipples heaving—smallish, up close they weren't so perky after all.

"Sit down on the floor with your back against the cabinets," I instructed. I removed my own clothing and sat between her legs, squeezing her beautiful, less-than-perfect breasts against my back and leaning my head against her shoulder. I could feel the movement of her throat as she swallowed, the deep breath she took to steady herself, the pressure of her pelvis arching into me as her hand snaked down between my legs.

Her fingers sent thrills through my body, but when she asked, "Does that feel good?" I chose not to answer. I wasn't going to help Ms. I-Can-Do-Anything with this do-it-yourself project; she'd have to figure it out on her own.

But I forgot that I had never had sex with a woman before. I forgot that, without ever touching me previously, she would know my body almost as well as I did. I didn't have to tell her that my clit got overjoyed when you snuck up on it from behind. I didn't have to tell her that more is not always better when it comes to deep-probing digits. And I sure as hell didn't even *know* to tell her about that fabulous thing she did with her thumb.

She already knew to play with my breast while her fingers fucked me. She knew to wrap her entire hand around the base and pull upward, tightening her grip until only her thumb and forefinger pinched my nipple as she tugged. She knew all the tricks, and she knew to do them all over again and again, in just the right intervals, until I had no breath left and my muscles tensed up tight and I exploded in savage waves against her hand.

It took a while for the room to stop spinning. I stumbled to stand on rubber legs and took her hand to pull her up. "Thank you," I whispered, pressing her against the counter, partly to kiss her and partly to keep from falling.

Flushed and pleased, Madison followed my directions to sit back up on the counter. The sight of her bare ass on the Formica made me giggle. "Blake always sets his dirty tumbler in that spot when he gets back from the coffee shop," I explained. "I don't think I'll ever wash this part of the counter again." My explanation didn't help Madison's confusion, but I distracted her by gingerly touching one fingertip to the small rise of her clit. Her breath whistled through her teeth and she pulled me close for a fierce kiss. I let my finger slip down along the warmth of her crease. When I added a second finger and slid them both slowly inside her body, Madison rocked back against the wall and closed her eyes. Her tongue peeked out, barely visible between parted teeth, and I could see her pulse hammering in her white throat.

Hooking my fingers up slightly, I stroked back and forth across her soft, grooved flesh. I could feel tremors of excitement shuddering up through her hips as I pulled and teased, pulled and teased, circling my thumb against her clit and savoring the delight of having Madison more or less at my mercy.

When her whistling breaths changed to agonized whimpers I decided I should give her some relief. I lowered my face between her legs and kissed her with the same enthusiasm I had given her lips. I didn't nibble her delicate flower or gently lick her lollipop or exercise any of the other half-assed, maddening efforts at oral sex that had been tried on me. I didn't tease or toy with her any longer. I dived in and devoured her cunt. I gave her the tongue-screwing I'd always wished for myself: hungry, grating, unrelenting. And I loved it. I loved the taste of her, the smell of her. I worked her pretty pink clit with my tongue and jaw until her shoulders shook against the back wall, her legs trembled against the counter and her whimpered pleas turned into gasping wails. She clutched and clawed at my hair as each suspended wave arched through her. Frankly, we were both quite impressed with ourselves.

After we'd taken a minute to catch our breath, Madison traced a wandering finger along my upper arm. "Change is good?" she asked. I leaned my head against her chest and thought about my recent turnaround change in attitude. "No doubt. Change looks pretty and shiny."

RUNNING AWAY AND RUNNING HOME AGAIN

Annabeth Leong

Kevin drove us back to his house after we got off our shifts at the restaurant, but I hesitated as he pulled into the driveway. "Maybe you should take me home," I said.

He parked and turned to me, dark face shaded darker by the shadow from the porch light. "Come on, Selma. I'll make you breakfast in the morning." He put his hand on my knee, slid it up under my skirt, and switched to Spanish. "*Jamon. Huevos. Te quiero.*"

I slapped at his hand, catching his fingers before they could get under my panties. "Okay. But wait until we get inside. I don't want your creepy roommate watching us."

"Dave? You didn't hear?" He pulled his hand out from under my skirt, dragging his nails along my inner thigh and laughing at my gasp. "His woman came home. They've been locked in the bedroom since yesterday morning. You've got nothing to worry about."

Kevin got out and came around the car to open the door for

me. "I thought you said she wasn't coming back," I said. He shrugged and pulled me up out of my seat and into a kiss.

"Let's just get inside," I said.

As soon as we opened the door, I heard her voice, moaning like I have never moaned. "I didn't know a woman could make sounds like that," I said.

"Is that a challenge?" Kevin asked, raising an eyebrow.

"I don't know about that."

He pulled me into his bedroom. "I want to hear you make those sounds," he said. "You just close your eyes and pretend you're Barbara."

I giggled and shook him off me. "That's weird," I said.

Kevin pushed me onto his bed, pulled my panties down and buried his face between my thighs with unusual vigor. I cried out in shock and heard an answering groan rising from Barbara. At the sound of her voice, a shiver went through my body, and my legs spread wider. "There you go," he said, and locked his lips around my clit.

I moaned back to her. She let out a series of sharp moans that I found myself imitating. My body moved to match the sounds we made. Kevin groaned at the same time as Dave, flipping me over and pounding his cock deep into me with one thrust. I turned my head to the side and kept up the conversation with her.

I pretended I was her. I imagined Dave behind me working me over with a thick, veiny prick. I screamed as I came. As my cunt continued to flutter around Kevin's cock, I tasted her name in my mouth and in my mind: Barbara.

Kevin fell asleep with his arm over my stomach, trapping me with its sticky length. We finished long before Barbara and Dave. For hours, I lay awake listening to her sighs, curses and sobs, trying to imagine what she looked like.

Sometime after midnight, the house went silent. A door down the hall opened and closed. I froze, realizing we'd left the door to Kevin's room open. The footsteps down the hall sounded light, so at least it wasn't Dave.

I saw her as she passed, a flash of creamy skin that seemed to glow in the night. Barbara was tall, completely naked, with thick black hair that fell halfway down her back. She stopped in the doorway and looked in on us. I snapped my eyes shut, heart pounding and body burning at the thought of her seeing me. The footsteps passed away a moment later, but I was afraid to open my eyes. Blood roared through every part of me until I fell asleep.

Kevin was gone in the morning. I rolled over in bed, feeling sticky, smelly and let down. Christ knew when he'd last washed his sheets. I opened one eye to check the time. I didn't have to be back at the restaurant until the dinner shift at three. Kevin must have forgotten what shift he had to work when he'd promised ham and eggs.

I hauled myself up out of bed and looked around for my clothes. I pulled my bra off the windowsill, retrieved my underwear from the shelf where he kept his Xbox, and found my top and skirt crumpled on a pile of unopened mail. I heard a creak from some other part of the house and realized the damn door was still open. I slammed the door shut even as I thought I heard a woman's laugh.

I dressed, pulled myself together as much as I could with the compact mirror in my purse, took a deep breath and went out to the kitchen.

"How are you getting home?" a familiar voice said. "The only car out there is mine."

I rounded the corner and saw her in the light for the first

time. Barbara leaned against the counter with a coffee cup in one hand, looking me up and down with a knowing expression. Her thick black hair curled slightly at the bottom and matched her eyes exactly. She was maybe five years older than me.

"Do you want breakfast?"

"I should get going."

"For Christ's sake. Sit down and have breakfast with me. I'll give you a ride home after."

I nodded. She fried eggs and bacon and poured coffee. My mind couldn't take in all of her. I would stare at her hands, then give up and shift to her shoulder or the nape of her neck. The silence between us began to stretch. I went ahead and asked, point blank. "Where did you go?"

She set a plate in front of me. "I thought Dave must have been telling everyone. You really don't know?"

I shook my head. "He didn't talk much about it to me."

Barbara's eyes drilled into mine. "I was with his best friend, Paul." She closed her eyes, looking older for a moment. "I knew it was going to kill Dave, but the sex was too amazing. That was all I wanted to do with that man. I lost ten pounds in two weeks, just from sex."

"Sounds like Dave plans to help you keep up the exercise program."

She smirked. "Doesn't have it in him, but he is trying." Barbara drained the rest of her coffee, not bothered by the heat. "Ten pounds," she repeated. "From sex."

"Why did you come back?"

A wrinkle appeared in her creamy forehead. "Dave called the house about three times a day. At first he made threats, and we laughed at them, but then he started sounding really pathetic. He'd call and beg for Paul to send me home, saying he just wanted everything to go back to the way it was before."

"And you couldn't handle it?"

The wicked glimmer came into her eyes again. Her full, pink lips puckered. "Paul couldn't handle it. He told me I had to go. I spent a couple weeks staying with a friend, and things got... wild. I got tired of it and decided to come home."

She shrugged lightly, as if to show that the devastation I'd seen in her wake hadn't really been all that heavy. I smiled nervously. I wondered if it could possibly be true she'd had enough sex in two weeks to lose ten pounds.

Barbara stood. "Hurry up and eat so we can get you home."

I rode my bike to Kevin's house the next Saturday. I didn't know his work schedule for sure, but if I had been honest with myself, I would have known he wasn't home. Barbara opened the door.

She studied me, seeming to inspect every sweat stain and blemish. I always felt I caught glimpses of some inner cruelty hidden behind her eyes. "You don't drive?" she said.

I shrugged. "Long story. But no, I don't. My license is suspended."

Barbara grinned. "Party girl? I wouldn't have known."

"I'm not a party girl anymore," I said, sighing. "If I'm good, I'll get my license back in another six months."

"Kevin's not home," Barbara said. "But you should come in."

Inside, three lawn-sized black trash bags dotted the living room, drooping and spilling their contents on the floor. I saw a studded leather collar, a pink sweater, and the kind of stuffed toy that comes out of a crane machine. "What's going on?" I said.

"Dave picked up my stuff from Paul's house today. I don't think anyone was killed. But I do think Dave's out drinking now." She gave an inappropriately hearty laugh.

"Need any help sorting through all this?"

"Actually, there are a bunch of clothes I was going to give away. Maybe you would want them."

"I don't know if they would fit," I said.

"I was your size before I was with Paul." She took me by the wrist. "Come try them on."

Dave and Barbara's room smelled sour with sex. The sheets had slipped half off the bed, and stains on the mattress showed this must have happened days ago without either of them bothering to fix it. Clothing had exploded all over the floor, and a dresser next to the bed leaned against the wall at a 45-degree angle. Barbara took in the damage with a secret, victorious smile.

She hefted another trash bag from the floor and spilled its contents onto the soiled bedspread. I looked up at her, startled.

"Jesus," Barbara said. "Don't be a grandmother. Try something on."

I touched the pile slowly. I couldn't discern any recognizable piece of clothing in the flimsy mass of sequins and netting before me. I lifted a bit of blue spandex and wondered where exactly it had gripped Barbara's body. "What do you suggest?"

She rolled her eyes and tossed me something gold. "This would look good against your skin." I caught it and hesitated. Barbara made an impatient hand gesture. I turned around and removed my shirt.

My whole body warmed as I felt her eyes on my back. I dropped the shirt somewhere in the sea of clothes and swallowed hard. Reaching back to undo my bra strap, I imagined my hands were her hands, and froze as I realized what I had been hoping for since I first learned Barbara's name. She stepped up behind me and brushed my hands out of the way.

I closed my eyes and moaned as she loosened my bra and it slid off my body. I leaned back against her. Barbara stopped and pushed me upright. "You are too much," she said. I couldn't read her tone. She unsnapped my skirt and yanked down my underwear. "You shouldn't be so shy," Barbara said, tugging at the gold fabric still in my hand. "Put this on."

I stepped into it, a ridiculous one-piece that began with a thong at the bottom, then continued with two thin straps traveling up the edges of my stomach to a wire that lifted my breasts but left them uncovered from the nipples up. It fastened with a tie around the neck. I stared down at myself, again imagining that my body was Barbara's. I wanted to touch myself all over.

"Are you going to let me see?" Barbara said.

I turned around. One of her eyebrows went up. I felt triumphant for a moment, until she burst out laughing. "I didn't know you don't shave," she gasped. I looked down at myself, seeing the thin gold strip of the thong lost within a forest of wiry black hairs.

All the blood that had been between my legs went up to my face and ears. I swallowed hard and pulled together as much dignity as I could. It was enough that I could take the garment off slowly and find my clothes on the floor before fleeing to Kevin's room. Barbara's laughter followed me down the hall.

Kevin came home from work and found me playing Xbox, shooting mutants in the head in Fallout 3. "I didn't know you were this good," he said.

"I wasn't until now," I said, focusing on another critical hit. "I've been playing since eleven a.m."

"What's the matter?" He sat next to me and put his arms around me. Grease spatters from the fryers at work had covered his forearms with little sores. "You mad they didn't put you on the schedule tonight?"

I rubbed my head against his tight black curls. "Nah, I let

Carole have my shift because she needs to make rent. I'm fine."

"You should tell me when you get a day off," he said. I knew why I hadn't told him, and whom I'd wanted to see. I put down the controller mid–critical hit. Kevin turned my head to face him and met my eyes a few seconds before nodding and pulling me to my feet.

He kissed me once, slowly, his lips full and sticky against mine. I kept my eyes open, gauging his reaction to me. He seemed wary and pulled back. "Want me to close the door?" he murmured.

I shook my head. "I don't think anyone else is home," I lied. I locked eyes with Kevin and slid my skirt down my hips, discarded my shirt. It was easier with him. I knew he'd be spellbound.

I pulled my bra straps down over my shoulders and rolled the cups down one at a time to tease him with flashes of nipple. Kevin grinned, stepping forward to touch me. Shaking my head, I steered him to sit at the foot of the bed so his back was to the doorway. My thumbs hooked into the waistband of my panties, rolling them down inch by inch.

"*Dios mio*," he breathed. "You shaved your pussy." He grabbed me and pulled me to him, running his hands over the new smoothness between my legs. The sensation on my sensitive skin was almost too much to bear. I gripped his shoulders and cried out.

Kevin leaned in and licked the fold at the top of my thigh, then licked across the skin to nip my clit, which stood out bright pink at the top of my cleft. I shrieked but snapped my head up at the sound of a creak in the hallway.

She stood in the doorway, leaning her head against the frame, a big grin on her face. I didn't want Kevin to see her there. I pushed him flat and sat on his face. He moaned some words I couldn't make out. His tongue pressed hard between my pussy lips, worked into my vagina, swirled a wet trail over the entire region between my thighs. I pretended it was hers. I gripped the top of Kevin's head and pulled him tighter against my cunt, and he groaned again.

In the doorway, Barbara reached for the buttons at the front of her dress and undid them one by one. She shrugged and the dress slipped to the floor. Underneath, she wore the gold outfit I had tried on earlier. I groaned and reached behind me for the button at the top of Kevin's jeans. He bit a little when I touched his straining cock. As soon as I freed his cock, I moved down his body and slammed my cunt down on his prick. Kevin let out a strangled cry, which I silenced with a kiss. I licked all over his mouth, tasting myself, then looked back up at Barbara.

She slipped a finger inside the thong, rubbing it against her clit. A moment later, she slid her finger between her lips. I changed my rhythm riding Kevin, slowing and curving the path of my hips so my clit pressed against his pelvic bone every time I took his length. My eyes glued to Barbara, I came. My body clenched around Kevin's cock so tightly that I had to close my eyes. I rippled there while he bucked frantically under me.

I opened my eyes when the orgasm passed, and Barbara was no longer in the doorway. I looked down at Kevin, who grunted and gasped as if this were the fuck of his life. Without her there, the excitement drained out of me. I watched his face as I waited for him to finish.

I didn't see Barbara again until the next Saturday when she invited me to party at a friend's house. Her eyes glinted with a mischief that made my guts churn.

"Where's Dave?"

"Honestly? I think he's out again. Maybe he's got another girlfriend."

"Why would he? You..." I trailed off.

Barbara laughed. "Now that I'm back, I don't matter anymore." She looked at me sideways. "Not to him, anyway."

It was a hot night, the air full of bugs. They congregated around the porch light, getting in the way as we got into Barbara's car. They spattered against the windshield as she drove and buzzed in my ears when we parked in her friend's driveway. Barbara opened the door to the house without knocking. I shrank from the wall of noise and smoke.

Every woman I saw wore a skimpy little costume. There was no shortage of men, dancing with the women, touching them. Raucous laughter rang in my ears, a thick layer of sound spread underneath a heavy dance music beat.

"You are so naïve," Barbara said. She took me by the wrist and pulled me through the crowded room to a chair in the corner. She turned me to face her and slowly wound her arms around my neck. She bent her head down to whisper in my ear. "How badly do you want me?"

It was an obvious question, but I didn't have the voice to answer it. I shook my head, feeling her hair against my cheek as I did.

"You don't want me?"

"I've never done anything like this before," I admitted. She made me feel small and pathetic. I wondered if Dave and Paul felt the same.

"You seemed like you knew what you were doing last week."

"I'm not here to get humiliated."

"Then do something about it. Give me a lap dance."

"In front of everyone?"

"In front of me," Barbara said. She sat in the chair, watching me with brazen challenge on her face.

"I'm not dressed for it."

"So take off your clothes," she said.

I did, ignoring the ring of silence that rippled out around me as people saw what we were doing and gathered to watch. I stripped down to my underwear, then thought *Fuck it* and stripped the rest of the way.

I stepped toward Barbara and straddled her. Already, my pussy felt so wet I was sure I would leave spots all over her jeans. I tried to dance somehow, but really the music was gone as soon as I looked into her eyes. I ran my breasts up either side of her face like I'd seen strippers do in movies, but she turned her head and licked one of my nipples as it passed.

I lost control of myself, grabbed her by the hair, and bolted my mouth onto hers. All thought went out of my mind except for raging need. I swept my tongue into her mouth, and then my hands were all over her, pinching her nipples, pawing at her breasts, working their way between her legs. I wanted her to scream my name. I wished I could fuck her with a huge cock until she forgot everyone she'd ever met before.

And then I was pushing her off the chair, tearing down her pants, wrenching her legs apart, and burying my face between them. I licked her pussy hard, and, when I couldn't hear her moaning, I put one finger and then another inside her. I stabbed four fingers into her as I sucked her clit. Her hips began to move under me, and I growled with satisfaction.

I swirled my forefinger around her asshole, and pressed slowly inside that, my own pussy thumping at every one of Barbara's sharp pants. My thumb in her vagina and my first finger in her ass, I squeezed them together as I raked my tongue across her bud.

She did say my name then, gasping out "Selma" as I felt her muscles begin to spasm around me. I didn't relent right away. I rode one set of spasms on up and through to the second orgasm. Only then did I take my cramping hand out of her body and look up to see the expression on her face.

Her cheeks were flushed. I kissed her again, slower this time, aching inside as I did it. If I thought of Kevin, it was only to note I didn't care. "Maybe I can make you lose fifteen pounds," I told her.

Around us, people started clapping. I remembered we had an audience. Someone helped me to my feet and tried to feel me up. I batted his hands away and turned back to Barbara. I wanted to ask if there was somewhere more private we could go.

It took me a minute to see her through the haze and confusion. When I spotted her, she was leaning against some man, sucking on a joint he held for her. She hadn't bothered to put her pants back on. I walked up to them. "Barbara," I began.

She bent to whisper in my ear again. "What do you think of him?" she asked, jerking her head toward a tattoo of a stylized sun that covered half his chest.

"I don't give a shit about him," I said, not bothering to lower my voice. "Can we get out of here?"

"You need to relax, Selma. You sound like Dave. Why don't we stay here and have some fun?"

It dawned on me then that it wasn't really me she wanted. The rage that passed through me in that moment shocked me. I backed away and retrieved my clothes. I found her pants, too, and took the keys out of the pocket. I considered having a drink, staying at the party, picking up someone else, but I was too angry to want any of those things. I went out to her car.

I wanted to drive until I forgot about her. I almost emptied the tank once, filled it up again, and kept driving. I hoped the cops would stop me and ask about my license. My whole life seemed like a crock to me then—the restaurant job, the months of sobriety, the boyfriend I fucked because I didn't know what else to do. I stopped the car and rolled the taste of her through my mouth.

In the morning, when I went to pick Barbara up, she lay asleep on the floor in the arms of the man with the sun tattoo. I stood there a long time, learning what I already knew, until I dropped the keys on the floor beside her and began the long walk home.

AN INTRODUCTION

G. G. Royale

Kalini stood at the threshold of the club and refused to enter.

Her fiancé, Hajar, pulled at her wrist. "Come on."

"I don't want to." She hadn't realized she would feel this anxious, but good Indian girls didn't visit bondage clubs—her mother's voice kept repeating it in her head. *What if mother really found out?*

"No sex in front of anyone tonight. I promise," Hajar told her.

"No. Take me home."

"You're not acting very submissive right now, Kalini," Hajar warned. "You should give in to your man more easily."

How her parents—thousands of miles away in India—could still control her life here, she had no idea. *Fucking arranged marriage.* She already knew she and Hajar were sexually incompatible. She'd given in so far to Hajar's...inclinations, but this felt utterly and completely wrong. "We could both ruin our careers if people saw us in there."

"They have very strict privacy policies. Now come on."

He pulled again, and Kalini lost her balance, tripping through the open door.

Inside the club, a heavy bass beat shook Kalini. Everything was either shiny chrome or glossy black, including most of the people's clothing. She looked down at her black dress, the motorcycle boots her nod to the edginess needed for the club. She didn't compare to other women wearing lingerie, vinyl catsuits, and risqué costumes.

"Please, Hajar," she said, placing a hand on his shoulder. "I want to go home."

"No."

He said it with authority. She would be here for the evening, then. She sighed and took Hajar's hand. He looked down at her. He could probably tell she'd finally given in. He smiled.

"This will be fun," he said, leading her to the bar.

Kalini saw nothing fun about this. It was one thing to let Hajar handcuff her to their brass headboard. She didn't even mind the spankings with the leather paddle he bought at the adult store. Sometimes, she could close her eyes and pretend he was someone...different, and then she actually enjoyed it. But here, in a club surrounded by people who obviously knew more about the scene, and the beautiful, tall American women with their bouncy hair and long legs, she felt tiny and completely inadequate.

They sat at the bar, and Hajar ordered her a drink. The bartender set it in front of her with a smile.

"Pretty little thing, aren't you?"

She took a breath and stared at the bar.

"Submissive, too, huh? You should get your Master to teach you how to take a compliment."

She could hear the teasing in his voice, but when she looked up at Hajar, he was scowling.

"Anybody want to co-Dom with me?" a voice called out in the club.

"I'll do it," Hajar leaped from his seat and raised his hand.

"Excellent." Another Dom, dressed in leather pants and nothing else, came over and shook hands with Hajar. "I'm Devin, by the way."

"Hajar and my fiancée, Kalini."

Devin towed a naked girl behind him on a leash. Kalini shook her head and sipped her drink. What did he intend to do with her?"

"Come on over to the spanking bench. I've got it reserved."

"I'll wait here," Kalini told Hajar.

"Don't go anywhere."

Some of the other submissives at the bar, ones left alone, had been chained to eyebolts so they couldn't leave.

She drank, listening to the music and the sounds of whips, chains and people moaning. *Maybe I should just leave,* she thought.

"Is this seat taken?"

Kalini turned and looked at the newcomer. The woman looked like Bondage Barbie. She stood nearly six feet tall, had huge blonde hair, and wore a leather corset and pencil skirt that clung to her every curve. Kalini thought back to the times she closed her eyes when Hajar spanked her. This was the someone else she fantasized about, right down to the stiletto heels. She could feel herself growing damp between her legs.

Kalini's mouth watered. *Dear Ganesha, what is wrong with me?* She'd never been with a woman, and now she sat here, contemplating one in the flesh as if the blonde were a financially successful software designer or a doctor. In her head, her mother screamed obscenities—well, as obscene as the minuscule woman ever got—and cursed Kalini for being unwholesome and perverted.

"Please s-sit." She took another huge sip of her drink, trying to get the mother voice in her head to shut up. Gin and tonic, not even something she really liked; it was another way Hajar liked to remind her he was boss. "Can I get a whiskey sour?" she asked the bartender, putting down her half-empty drink.

Barbie sat down and ordered herself a shot of tequila. "I'm Leila, by the way."

"Kalini," she said.

The bartender set the drinks down, and Kalini took a long sip. Her mother's voice receded to a tolerable drone.

"I see you're not chained," Leila said. "Do you have a Domme for the evening?"

"I'm here with my fiancé." Kalini turned in her seat and surveyed the room. She saw Hajar. The other Dom had bent the sub over a bench; he fucked her from behind, and Hajar had his cock in her mouth. Kalini's stomach soured. She couldn't believe he'd break a promise so easily. She looked at Leila. "But he's doing something else now, so no, I don't have anybody tonight."

With those words, she knew she damned herself, but right now, she didn't care. If Hajar got to give in to his fantasy, she would give in to hers.

"Wonderful." Leila smiled, filling Kalini with warmth. The wetness between her legs intensified. "Your safeword is ginger; I'd like to try you out on a table, if you don't mind."

"Sounds good to me." Kalini smiled and stood.

"You must address me as 'Ma'am' when you speak to me." Leila took her tequila off the bar and threw it back. She clutched Kalini's wrist with her other hand. Kalini gazed up at the taller woman, and she could feel—even with only the glances and this touch—her arousal building, unlike anything she'd ever felt for Hajar. Leila leaned down and brushed a kiss across Kalini's lips. It was a soft but lingering introduction, and Kalini couldn't suppress her grin.

"Come." Leila pulled Kalini across the floor toward a tall table padded in purple leather. Restraining points studded the sides. This would be much more interesting than handcuffs at home.

And she would be in front of people. Kalini had gotten waxed yesterday, had plucked and shaved herself into submission. She knew—despite the fact she didn't resemble some of these Amazonian goddesses—she looked good. Nevertheless, she'd never appeared in public like this.

"Strip," Leila commanded. The tone of her voice left no room for argument. She might have been able to say no to Hajar in this situation but certainly not Leila. She had something Kalini wanted, and Kalini knew now she would do anything to get it.

She removed her boots, then her dress, and finally she took of her underwear. Leila walked around her.

"Very nice," she said. "Now on the table."

Kalini climbed on the table. She didn't know how Leila wanted her. "In what position, Ma'am?" she asked.

"On your back."

Kalini lay on her back and waited.

"Tell me if anything is too tight or uncomfortable." Leila went to work.

First, she cuffed Kalini's wrists, clipped them together, and attached them to a point over her head.

Next, a strap went across her chest, and Kalini felt the first niggles of doubt in her stomach. She hadn't asked what Leila intended to do to her once she was secured to the table. The woman could do anything, really, including letting other people touch or molest her. Kalini knew she didn't want that. She only wanted Leila.

Safeword. She had a way out. She just needed to remember it.

Cuffs went around her thighs, and Leila secured those with

short straps to the sides of the tables. Then her ankles were cuffed as well, and Leila moved Kalini's knees and clipped the ankle cuffs to the thigh cuffs. Kalini's legs were spread wide, her knees in the air. She couldn't move. She didn't want to.

Leila left and returned moments later. She had removed her skirt and covering her sex was an elaborate harness system graced with a massive strap-on. Kalini felt more nervous now. The dildo seemed far larger than anything she'd ever seen in her limited experience.

"Ma'am, I don't know that I can—"

"You can when I've prepared you." Leila came to the table and stroked Kalini's cheek. "Don't doubt yourself so easily."

Kalini nodded and stared at the ceiling. People had gathered around to watch, and she wanted to try her best to block them out. She wanted to pretend only Leila remained in the room with her.

Kalini glanced at Leila then. The woman climbed onto the table between Kalini's legs. Kalini swallowed as Leila approached, her gaze predatory. She stopped, her mouth just inches from Kalini's pussy.

"I'm going to lick you until you come. Then I'm going to fuck you like a man."

Kalini gasped, and Leila smiled as she dipped her head to Kalini's sex. First came a lick. Then Kalini felt the long, sharp nails of Leila's fingers rake up and down the flesh of her thigh. Kalini pulled against her restraints, wanting to grab Leila's head and force her to eat her out and stop the teasing. Leila's tongue brushed to the left and right of Kalini's clit but kept avoiding it. It was a delicious torture. Kalini squirmed, barely able to move an inch but trying desperately to get Leila to lick her properly.

Finally, Leila took a swipe at Kalini's clit, and Kalini cried out. She wanted more. Leila's fingers slipped into Kalini's cunt, and Kalini rose up the few centimeters she was allowed to meet the invasion. She wanted it hard and fast, but Leila kept it slow and teasing.

"Anybody looking can tell how wet you are," she whispered against Kalini's skin.

"Please, Ma'am, make me come," Kalini begged.

Leila chuckled and started licking Kalini's clit again and sliding her fingers in and out of Kalini's cunt. Kalini writhed on the table. She wanted to pinch her nipples but couldn't. One touch there would send her off. Hell, even just thinking about fingers or lips plucking and sucking at her nipples...

"Ahhh!" Kalini came, the orgasm shuddering through her body like an express train. She cried out again as Leila continued to lick and nip at her clit, her pussy, the skin of her thighs.

"Now, you will take me," Leila said. She crawled up Kalini's body and lowered herself, first to lick Kalini's nipples, then her lips.

Kalini could taste herself on the other woman, like mango and young coconut. She licked at Leila's lips and darted her tongue between them. Kalini wanted to taste, to consume, to be a part of the exotic blonde Domme.

"Are you ready?" Leila asked.

"Oh, yes, Ma'am."

The giant silicone cock parted her pussy lips and squeezed inside. Kalini hissed as she was overcome by the feeling of being so filled.

Leila sighed, her breath fluttering Kalini's hair and lashes. "I have plugs buried in my own cunt and ass," she told Kalini. "Every stroke affects me as well. And your cunt tasted so good, I don't think it will take me long to come, but you must come again for me. Do you understand?"

"Yes, Ma'am."

The dildo continued to inch deeper until Kalini could feel the straps of the harness rubbing against her tender flesh.

Leila stayed like that for a moment before she started thrusting. Her strokes were fluid, like the movements of a ballet dancer rather than the jackhammering that Hajar favored. Kalini watched Leila's body above her, watched the dildo sliding in and out of her stretched lips. She thought about the plug in Leila's ass and wondered what that would feel like. She thought she might like to try it sometime.

She thought about hands on her breasts and fingers in her ass and the beautiful woman above her. She felt the dildo filling her, pushing her onward. Another orgasm gathered in that space below her belly, mustering like an army of sensation ready to make the final charge.

Leila's lips came down on hers in a savage assault. Kalini gave in to it. Her mind stopped. She felt only her cunt and her lips and the cuffs keeping her still, the friction of the straps creating a luscious burn that only intensified her need. Leila's thrusts became more adamant: short, quick drives.

"Come for me," Leila demanded. Her words pushed Kalini over the edge again.

Leila's call joined her own, and it seemed all other movement and noise around them ceased as they came together.

They lay like that for a while, Leila's warm weight making Kalini feel secure and satisfied. The other woman didn't pull out and leave for the shower like Hajar did. She rested there, her nose in the crook of Kalini's neck.

Finally, she got up and unstrapped Kalini. Kalini's legs wobbled, but Leila's strong hands held her until she steadied herself. She dressed slowly, her muscles stiff and resistant.

"I hope I see you again," Leila said. "Next time, you will kneel before me and eat *my* pussy."

She walked off into the crowd.

"What the fuck was that?" Hajar demanded as he emerged from the audience. "You said no sex."

"You were doing it, too." Kalini started for the door.

"But—"

She turned on him, her mind made up in an instant. "Cancel my ticket to Mumbai. The wedding is off. And find somewhere else to fucking live."

Hajar stopped dead in his tracks.

In one night, her world had turned upside down. She had destroyed an arranged marriage, her mother would disown her, and she had paraded naked in front of dozens of people. She was not the Kalini who had woken up this morning and put on her pantsuit to work at the advertising agency. She had become a different woman. Outside the club, the evening air felt crisp and cool. Kalini welcomed the sensation on her heated body and headed for home.

SEDUCTION BY PROXY

Evan Mora

Jeanine's my best friend, has been since high school. Back then it was passing notes in math class and soccer practice after school, breaking down who said what to who and talking about boys. Then one day in senior year she says, "Heather, I'm a lesbian."

I didn't see that one coming. Jeanine's looking at me like she's waiting for me to be all grossed out, but I don't care about that kind of stuff. I shrug like it's nothing and say, "So I guess now we've gotta talk about girls too, huh?"

Jeanine smiles like it's Christmas and just about knocks me down with the biggest hug ever. Then she pulls back just a little and brushes her lips against mine. *Really* didn't see that one coming.

I say, "You might like the girls, but I still like the boys, okay?"

She looks a little crestfallen but picks herself up like only Jeanine can and shrugs.

"Yeah, okay. We still good?"

"Always."

And we always have been. We bunked together in college, playing varsity soccer and pulling too many all-nighters, studying and eating pizza and talking about the trouble with guys and the perils of girls. Then one night we drink too much and Jeanine says to me, "Heather, haven't you ever wondered why all my girlfriends look like you?"

I can't say I hadn't noticed Jeanine's penchant for girls with long dark hair, blue eyes and pale skin like mine, but I'd been content to leave the subject alone. Jeanine moves closer to me on the couch and runs her fingers through my hair.

"Jeanine..." I begin, but she doesn't let me finish. She leans in and catches my mouth with hers, kissing me like a lover and pressing her body against mine. She tastes like wild berry coolers and she's so very, very soft, and it would be easy to do this thing that she wants, but...

"You know this isn't going to happen," I say, pulling away.

"It could if you let it."

"You're my best friend."

"I could be more."

"Jeanine!" I exclaim. There's a beat of silence. We stare at each other. She sighs and brushes her sandy blonde curls off her shoulders with a wistful smile.

"Can't blame a girl for trying," she says.

"Besides," I say, passing her another drink. "You're forgetting one minor detail."

"Oh, yeah, what's that?"

"I still like the boys."

Jeanine snorts in a decidedly unladylike fashion.

"What makes you think a boy is so much better than a girl, huh?"

"What can I say," I tell her with a shrug, "I like a nice hard cock."

Jeanine laughs outright.

"Oh, Heather," she says. "What makes you think I don't?"

We rent an apartment together after university and spend most of our time working. She dates. I date. Neither of us has much time for a serious relationship so the names and the faces of the guys and the girls all kind of blend together. Until Cary.

Cary doesn't look like the girls Jeanine usually dates, which is to say, she doesn't look like me—at all. Cary's got a swimmer's body—strong shoulders and slim hips; she's hardly got any curves to speak of. Cary has a messy blonde fauxhawk that always looks like she's just crawled out of bed. A bed she's been fucking in. I can't stop staring at her.

Jeanine and I have always kept our sexual escapades behind our respective closed doors, but it's like her brain short-circuits with Cary. I come out of my room for a glass of water and Jeanine's up on the counter with her legs wrapped around Cary's waist, moaning into the other woman's mouth and grinding her crotch against Cary's jeans. I don't even think they see me.

I come home from work and Jeanine's straddling Cary's lap on the sofa, her head thrown back and her eyes closed as Cary kneads her breasts and nips at her neck seductively. Cary sees me watching from where I'm frozen just inside the door and winks at me. I blush a furious red and retreat to my bedroom, slamming the door behind me, tingling in places I don't want to tingle.

It's no better when they *are* behind closed doors. Jeanine's headboard sounds like it's going to break through the thin wall separating our rooms. The unmistakable sounds of bodies coming together and sweating and giving in to noisy orgasms becomes an insidious soundtrack that steals into my subconscious and torments my dreams.

I stumble to the bathroom one morning after another

near-sleepless night and there's a cock sitting on the counter, a big one. There's a big peach-colored cock strapped into a black leather harness sitting on my bathroom counter. I am indignant. Or, at least, I feel like I should be indignant. In truth, imagining Cary wearing this cock is incredibly arousing. Imagining what she can do with it turns me on even more.

"Great," I mutter to my reflection. "Just great. I'm lusting after my best friend's lover. My *lesbian* best friend's *female* lover. Who just happens to have a giant cock. What the hell am I supposed to do about that?" My reflection offers no advice.

I scrub my way through a brisk shower and get ready for work before heading to the kitchen for a quick bite. They are sitting at the table, looking disgustingly well fucked. Jeanine's wearing a little pair of baby doll pajamas. Her hair is a wild tangle of curls. Cary's wearing what look like a pair of boxer briefs and a tight-fitting vintage rock T-shirt that show off her lean thighs and flat stomach. Not that I'm looking.

They're sharing a plate of waffles with maple syrup and Cary's feeding Jeanine, placing tiny morsels between Jeanine's swollen lips while Jeanine moans with pleasure. A drop of syrup trails down Jeanine's chin and Cary leans in, lapping up the sticky sweet with her tongue.

"For crying out loud, get a room!" I snap, downing my coffee too fast and burning my tongue. The sated duo look up at me lazily. I turn to the sink, running myself a glass of cold water.

"And put some clothes on," I add over my shoulder as their chairs scrape against the linoleum.

The next thing I know, Cary's arm brushes past my waist and her warm hard body is pressed up against my back.

I jump at the unexpected contact, a jolt of arousal running through me.

"Relax, Heather," Cary's breath whispers across my cheek,

"I'm just putting the plates in the sink." The clatter of said plates into the sink seems to corroborate her story, and her arm retreats as she steps away from me.

I turn around in time to see the two of them exchange a look I can't decipher before they disappear back into Jeanine's room.

I try earplugs, sleeping with a pillow over my head, relaxing meditations on my iPod; earsplittingly loud, angry music on my iPod. Nothing works. Nothing can drown out the sound of them fucking or the images in my head. I get aroused just hearing Jeanine's bedroom door click shut. My dreams are filled with a thousand filthy fantasies all centered around Cary.

I'm lying on my bed, staring at the ceiling, when the sounds begin again. First the moaning, then the slow beat of the head-board against our shared wall, a thrumming that increases both in volume and in speed in time with Jeanine's rising moans.

"That's it."

I'm off my bed and into the hall before I can question my actions. They've got to go. They've got to get out. Surely Cary has an apartment somewhere. If they don't go now, I will go crazy. I make to knock on Jeanine's door, but it isn't shut tightly. I find myself instead pushing it wide open and hungrily watching Cary drive her cock into Jeanine's welcoming pussy.

Whatever I'd imagined I might say flies out of my head as lust hits me square in the solar plexus. Watching the two of them fuck is the hottest thing I've ever seen, their bodies moving together sinuously, smooth skin sliding over smooth skin. It takes a moment to realize they're both watching me, though they haven't stopped doing what they're doing.

"I, uh...that is...your door's open," I stammer lamely, reaching for the doorknob as though my intention had been to close the door all along.

Cary withdraws, raising herself up so that she's kneeling between Jeanine's thighs, wet cock jutting like a heavy erection, her small breasts with their tight nipples a juxtaposition that floods my body with arousal. She holds a hand out to me.

"Why don't you come over here and suck my cock?"

No subtleties, no seduction—or maybe that's what this has been all along—but I'm crossing the floor, sliding my hand into hers, joining them on the bed and abandoning any pretense that this isn't exactly what I want.

Cary kisses me, and her lips are soft, the way I remember Jeanine's lips feeling—Jeanine who's now pressed against my back sliding her hands beneath my T-shirt and kneading my breasts while her own press sensuously against my back. Cary pulls my T-shirt over my head and resumes kissing me, her tongue snaking into my mouth, stealing the moan I can't stop when her breasts touch mine and Jeanine's hard nipples skate across my naked back.

Cary's cock presses insistently against my pelvis and Jeanine's hand slides around my waist and beneath my pajama pants, searching out the arousal that overflows from me and mingles with the heavy scent of sex already thick in the air. She strokes a finger through my wetness and circles my clit, whispering in my ear, telling me how beautiful I am.

Cary's hand is on my neck, stroking the sensitive skin and sending shivers of pleasure through me. She ends our kiss and gives me a slow smile, her hand guiding me now, pushing me down until my lips kiss the tip of her cock and my tongue swirls around its head, lapping the moisture Jeanine has left there. Jeanine feeds Cary my own wetness, sucked from her fingers and passed from her tongue to Cary's, a heady kiss feasting on my arousal.

My lips slide over Cary's cock, taking her into my mouth. The weight and feel of her are familiar yet different, though the way she moans and the helpless way her hips rock forward tell me she feels me just the same.

Jeanine draws my pajama pants down over my ass, past my thighs, as far as she can in my kneeling position, and I tense just a little, aware of how exposed I am; aware of the step I am taking; aware that things will never, ever be the same. Jeanine presses her warm lips to the small of my back, and then she slides her fingers inside me and it feels so damn good I can't think of anything but her moving in and out of me. I moan against Cary's cock, pressing my ass back into Jeanine as she increases her tempo, my muscles clenching around her fingers as Cary's hand tightens in my hair and she thrusts into my mouth, whispering to me, telling me how good I feel, telling me how pretty my lips look stretched around her cock.

Jeanine stops fucking me, but only so she can dispose of my pants entirely and nudge my knees farther apart. She positions herself beneath me and her warm breath between my thighs is all the warning I have before her tongue strokes from the back of my pussy to my aching clit, sending a spasm of pleasure rocketing through me. She grips my thighs with her hands, drawing me to her so that I'm all but sitting on her face as she gorges on me, lapping and sucking and moaning.

Cary slides her cock out of my mouth and pulls me upright once more, kissing my swollen lips, rolling the tight peaks of my nipples between her fingers. Jeanine's tongue is doing something divine to my clit. I want to come so badly I'm practically panting into Cary's mouth. She sits back on her heels, appraising me through heavy-lidded eyes, still pinching my nipples, watching the flush creep over my skin and the tremors of my mounting orgasm build.

"I want to fuck you," she says. "I want to bury my cock in you and fuck you until you come."

"Yes," I gasp, though if she doesn't do it soon, I'm going to come all over Jeanine's face, which feels like a pretty good option right now.

Jeanine slides out from beneath me and rises on her knees beside me, running her hands over my body possessively, my belly, my breasts, my still-swollen lips. She wraps her arms around my neck and kisses me deeply like she did so long ago, her body pressed tightly against mine, tongue sliding into my mouth. This time my mouth opens beneath hers, my tongue stroking against hers. She presses me backward without breaking the kiss, guiding me down until I'm lying on my back and she's stretched on top of me.

Cary joins the fray, the three of us kissing and stroking, writhing together in a hungry tangle of limbs until we reach a fever pitch and move by unspoken agreement, Cary positioning herself between my thighs, pressing the head of her cock into my pussy even as Jeanine settles herself above my mouth and I breathe in her arousal, stroking my tongue along her slit, then pushing inside. Jeanine moans against Cary's mouth, the two of them kissing as Cary sinks deeper into me, filling me, fucking me.

We're working ourselves to one of those heaving, sweating, noisy orgasms I've been hearing for weeks from my lonely bed on the other side of the wall, only this time I'm at the center of it all, my face buried in Jeanine's pussy, my hands clamped on her trembling thighs as she spasms and cries out above me a heartbeat before my own climax tears through me, Cary's cock driving me to unbelievable release even as she reaches her own shuddering end.

We collapse on the pillows, a mess of bodies trying to catch our breath, giving soft kisses and contented smiles, lazy hands still gently exploring new territories. Then someone's breath catches and everything stills, shifts and starts all over again.

Long story short, I don't think I'll ever lose my affection for a nice hard cock but I like the girls, too—clever Jeanine. Clever, clever girl.

DISCOVERING DONNIE

Cheyenne Blue

On a good day—and there were a few—she could pass for thirty-five, although she was the far side of forty. Subtle makeup, careful dressing over her long, lean body, and hair tinted to hide the first silver strands all gave her elegance and poise. Jodie was a legal secretary and had worked for Hartmann and Flesch since leaving school. No college, but she was smart and tough and made her way in the firm, doing her job, content to be background scenery in the cutthroat legal world. She worked hard, stayed late without complaint, and molded herself into the efficient automaton that was so prized within the firm.

After work each day, she walked home to her small apartment on the wrong side of Broadway. Sometimes she'd stop for a glass of wine in the Art Deco jazz bar on the way. It was usually deserted at that hour, and she'd sit on its black vinyl couch and let her mind wander in a way it couldn't in the prim and correct world of Hartmann and Flesch.

The day Jodie met Donnie was the day the litigation partner

closed the door of his office and told her that from now on she would be working for him. A promotion, she was told: more money, longer hours.

She made the appropriate restrained noises of appreciation, but when she walked home that night it was with the sinking feeling of things gone wrong. Since when had work defined her life? Was there nothing else? When her head cleared, she realized she was far from the jazz bar; indeed she was nearly at her apartment. The need for a glass of wine was strong but there was no liquor store nearby and she didn't have wine at home. She hesitated for a moment, then marched resolutely to the small brick bar on the corner of Louisiana and Eighth. She'd passed it often, but the only windows were too high to see into, and it always had a quiet unwelcoming look. Still, she needed that glass of wine, so she hitched her purse higher on her shoulder and stepped through the doors.

Inside was cozier than she anticipated. There was a curved bar in one corner, a pool table, and a jukebox that was currently playing Garth Brooks. Plates of sausage and buffalo wings sat on the counter; she'd arrived during happy hour.

Jodie spotted a vacant stool at the end of the counter and worked her way through the cluster at the bar to reach it. It seemed to be a workingman's pub; construction workers in shorts and singlets rested feet on the bar rail, a few men with their names embroidered on their clothing played pool, and a scattering of women in casual office wear gossiped at a table. She slid onto the last stool, ordered her glass of chardonnay, and reached for a buffalo wing.

That was when she met Donnie.

She barely registered him at first. His well-muscled bulky body and a head of thick brown hair were all she noticed. But when her hand brushed his arm while reaching for the wings, the unexpected frisson that shot through her made her pause. That zing of arousal—too long since she'd felt that—made her eyes shoot to the person who'd inspired it.

Donnie, although she didn't know his name then, pushed the wings within her reach.

"Thanks," she murmured, and her wine arrived —two brimming glasses.

"I only ordered one," she said, but the barman pointed to the 2-4-1 DURING HAPPY HOUR sign behind the bar.

Picking up the first, she drained half of it in one long swallow.

Donnie watched her. "Bad day?"

"Yeah. You could say." She stabbed a sausage with a cocktail stick, envisaging the litigation partner's smug face.

Donnie hitched his stool closer. His sturdy thigh brushed her leg, and once again, she marveled at the feeling the innocuous touch produced.

"Wanna tell me about it?"

She looked at him and the half smile and sincerity in his face convinced her. Besides, she wanted to vent her indignation, and there was no one else.

"I got a promotion."

"Must be more to it if you're not happy."

"There's more to life than work."

"Like?"

"Travel. Sport. Hobbies." She looked him full in the face. "Romance."

She caught herself. That was probably the wrong thing to say. It made her seem needy. But he didn't seem to mind. His eyes were on her face and she could see his appreciation.

"What will your husband say about that?"

Very unsubtle, but she didn't mind; his interest buoyed her.

"No husband," she said succinctly, and drained the first wine, pulling the second in front of her.

"Boyfriend? Partner? Live-in lover?" He hesitated. "Girl-friend?"

"None of those." She glanced at him over the wine, well aware that things were moving quickly, too quickly. It had been a long time.

He smiled. "Let me buy you dinner and you can tell me about it. A problem shared, and all that."

Jodie searched his face for the mark of the rapist or serial killer—not that she knew what she was looking for—but his open-faced sincerity reassured her. "That would be nice."

She drained her wine and slid off the stool. Donnie threw a couple of notes on the counter and gestured for the door. She noted he was shorter than she, but stocky and well put together, with a flat stomach underneath the plain white tee, and faded denims clinging lovingly to his muscular thighs. She briefly thought she should let a friend know where she was going. She shouldn't be going out at all on a weeknight when she had to be up early for work. Instead she said, "I'm Jodie."

"Donnie," he said, and opened the door for her, a gesture as old-fashioned as it was endearing.

He took her to a backstreet Mexican café, a homey place she had sometimes passed. Over enchiladas and green chili, she told him about her work and the promotion with longer hours.

Donnie scratched his chin. "What would happen if you simply refused?"

"I think I'd find myself out of a job."

"Is the job worth it?"

"No," she said, simply, and her breath caught as he covered her hand with his own, rough finger pads passing over her skin in a swift caress.

"Then 'no' it should be." He glanced at his watch—a simple chunky thing with a battered face. "I'm going to have to take you home now, Jodie. I have to be at work early tomorrow."

She knew she should be relieved that he wasn't expecting anything from her but a small—okay, a large—part of her was sorry. She'd been expecting the pass, the kisses, the fumbles, the whispered entreaty to let him come up *for coffee*.

"I have to work too," she said.

Donnie escorted Jodie back to her apartment, reaching past her to release the door of the pickup.

"I like you, Jodie," he said. "Would you come out for dinner again sometime?"

"That would be nice," she said, and then he kissed her.

It was a swift, short passing of his lips rather than a kiss that would lead to more, but her stomach somersaulted at the touch of his firm mouth. She wanted to pull him to her and feel his agile tongue, find out how his skin felt beneath her hands.

"Tomorrow?"

She nodded.

"Come to the bar again after work."

The next day at work, she barely registered her new boss. Her head was full of Donnie: how he'd looked, how he'd tasted in that short, sweet sip; the fresh, clean smell of him. The litigation partner looked at her appraisingly, but she was oblivious. She was counting down the hours and minutes to five thirty.

Just after six, she walked into the bar again. She'd considered going home to change into jeans but had reasoned that Donnie had seen her in work clothes yesterday, and besides, going home would take the best part of an hour. She couldn't wait that long to see him.

He was seated at the bar, a hefeweizen and two white wines in front of him. Jodie's eyes lingered, tracing his body with her eyes, seeing how his strong hands caressed the frosted glass of his pint. How would they feel tracing her body?

She slid onto the stool next to him. Immediately he cupped the back of her head, pulling in for a kiss.

Jodie's nights fell into a pattern. They met at the bar for happy hour. Two wines, buffalo wings for appetizers, and then they ate at small backstreet cafés—Mexican, Thai, Japanese, a family diner and back to the little Mexican café Jodie now thought of as *their place*. Every night, a kiss and he would leave her on her doorstep. No more, no less.

She was obsessed with Donnie. She woke with the feel of his skin beneath her hands and when she realized he was only in her dreams, her fingers would curl with his absence until her nails dug into her palms. She was distracted at work and made mistakes with papers, left court documents unsigned. She was reprimanded, but she didn't care. The litigation partner smiled to himself; he had made a mistake promoting her, but her inefficiency would make it easier to rescind the offer.

Jodie didn't know why Donnie didn't take her to bed. He'd come up to her apartment for a *cup of coffee* once, and it had been just that: a cup of coffee. She was sure he wanted her: the drugging heat of his kisses, the way his arms trembled as he held her told her so, and once she'd felt his erection against her leg. But he never asked, "Can I stay?" He had never tried to waltz her into the bedroom, had never slid his hands over her body in a proprietary way, even though she wanted him to. Oh, how she wanted him to.

She made a decision. On Friday, when he dropped her home, and after his customary kiss, when he said, "Tomorrow night?" she replied, "Only if you'll stay the night."

He drew back and traced her cheek with his finger. "If that's what you want, Jodie. If that's what you really want."

She nodded. "Do you ?"

"Oh, yes," he breathed, and the space between them was suddenly tense and molten with promise.

She dressed with care on Saturday: lacy boyshorts and matching bra, jeans worn soft with age that hugged her ass and flattened her stomach, a Western shirt and cowboy boots. She left her hair loose and it curled to her shoulders.

When she reached the bar, she saw that while she had dressed down, Donnie had dressed up. His jeans were black, his shirt pristine white, and he wore a bolo tie with a silver and turquoise clasp accenting his swarthy skin and sleek brown hair. There was no happy hour on Saturdays, so they left immediately, and Donnie turned the pickup toward the more genteel suburbs, away from the local cafés they usually visited.

"We going up market?" she teased.

"You're worth it." He squeezed her hand lightly and withdrew.

Donnie took her to a steakhouse, and they ate butter-soft filet and baby vegetables. Jodie's vision was filled with Donnie: his voice, his hands, how he met her eyes, and the thought of how he would feel inside her later.

They drank red wine and lingered over dessert, even when Jodie was so aware of every movement he made, every touch of his fingers to her hand, that her skin felt like a living canvas, stroked and lighted by his touch. But when the waiter offered coffee, she couldn't stand it any longer and refused.

Donnie picked up the tab, and they walked to his pickup. Drawing her into its hulking shadow under the streetlight, he stroked her face once more.

"You sure?"

"Yes."

She expected seduction and soft, tender words. Donnie was considerate, and she thought his lovemaking would be... respectful, controlled but ardent.

Inside her apartment Jodie found him staring at her with undisguised hunger. She went to him, wrapping her arms around his neck, slanting her mouth over his.

He devoured her. The control and restraint were gone, evaporated into the humid air. His tongue smoothed a pathway into her mouth and his fingers made their own explorations over her body.

Jodie thought briefly of the neatly laid tray for coffee and brandy in the kitchen—no time, no need. She responded to his ardor with her own passion. His body was hard and muscled beneath her hands, and when he pressed his hips into hers, she felt the insistence of his erection against her belly. *Oh, my.* He was hard and ready for her, and a rush of liquid heat coiled through her belly.

When Donnie plucked at the hem of her shirt, she pulled away, unfastening the buttons and letting it slide from her shoulders. The heat and appreciation in his eyes warmed her, and she continued, removing the lacy bra she'd chosen for him with such care, then sliding her jeans down her legs.

Donnie dropped to his knees, his arms around her waist and his cheek pressed to her belly. Jodie wound her fingers into that thick brown hair and held him there, feeling his arms enclosing her so tightly. Donnie shifted and pressed his mouth over the lace of her boyshorts. The heat of his breath reached her skin through the lace. And then Donnie's fingers were pulling down the lace, and his nose bumped her pubic bone and all she could see was the top of his head as he buried his face in her curling pubes. He parted her with careful fingers, and she thought she would faint with the pleasure of anticipation as he hovered for a moment before pressing his mouth to her pussy, his tongue sweeping in and around and over. An agile tongue stroked the side of her clit in flat, broad movements, then flickered over the tip with such a light feathering touch that her knees buckled.

Donnie's hands supported the backs of her thighs. "Easy now," he said, his words muffled by flesh and hair. Then he was lifting her onto his mouth, pulling her into him, subsuming her while his tongue and lips worked their magic.

One part of her wanted him to stop, open his zipper and push into her so that she knew what he felt like. Another, greater part, wanted him to stay there on his knees with his mouth melded to her pussy until she fractured into a million shining pieces. The decision wasn't hers to make. Donnie was in control, and as he suckled her, as his tongue flickered and darted, she knew she was going to come so hard her atoms would be spread around the room with the force of her implosion. Her knees buckled, she grabbed at his hair, and then in a keening wail the ripples built to a crescendo and she came in jerks of ecstasy, huge gulping spasms that left her belly sore and her pussy swollen and wet as a monsoon.

With shaking hands she tucked her damp hair behind her ears and reached for him, pulling him up along her body until she could kiss his salty lips. Then she reached for him, shucking his white shirt—not so pristine now— and kissing the small and shapely breasts she found beneath, running her hands firmly over his abs, tracing their definition.

"Jodie," he whispered, his breath coming fast and hot. "You know that—"

"Sssh," she soothed him, and stroked the curve of his breast, bending to take his nipple between her lips.

She contemplated letting him take her against the door, on the table, somewhere were it would be fast and hard and furious, but in the end she led him to her bed, where the light pooled in soft golden circles.

There she undid his jeans, pushing them down over his hips, then the white jockey shorts, until his cock stood free. She traced the straps that held it in place, learning how it was held there, then let her fingers drift along its jutting length, before finally dipping lower, and using her own anatomy as a guide, she stroked in a delicate touch.

Donnie jerked in surprise, hissed through his teeth.

"You don't want this?" she asked. "Let me make you come before you fuck me."

"It's not that," he said. "It's—"

"Shh," and she cut him off with a kiss. "Later. Tell me later."

"Later then," he replied, and emboldened, she redoubled her efforts, her fingers walking pathways so familiar, yet so strange.

He didn't come. Although his body shuddered, and her fingers were drenched with his juices, he controlled himself tightly. Abruptly, Jodie found herself pushed back on the bed, and Donnie hovered over her, his muscular body above hers. Instinctively, she parted her thighs, wanting him inside.

He didn't disappoint. She reached down to guide him, taking the warm shaft, maneuvering it so that the tip slid between her wet pussy lips. Her fingers dug into his buttocks so fiercely she felt the warm wetness of blood.

Donnie slid home with one sure, hard thrust, and then they were fucking, the bang and crash of a fierce coupling, the thrust and withdrawal. Her pussy clasped him, clenching around his hard pole, and the tightness and welling of sensation deep within told her she'd be coming again.

She didn't know if he could come like this, and she wanted to wait for him, but as he thrust even harder, she knew, with a sense of helpless fatality, she couldn't wait. He had her that much out of control. As she spasmed around him, she saw Donnie, his face contorted and red with effort, muscles rigid. When he collapsed on top of her, sliding over her in the sheen of their combined sweat, she realized from his breathing that yes, he'd come.

Donnie was too much of a gentleman to crush her, though she could have stayed forever in his arms. He rolled away, swooping back to kiss her, one of his hard, probing, drowning kisses, the sort that had made her fall for him in the first place.

There was an ease in his eyes that had been absent before their lovemaking.

"You knew," he said, simply.

"I guessed. Did I do it right?"

He laughed, a deep, tender chuckle. "Honey, there is no wrong way." He hesitated. "But you're not into men like me."

"Honey, I'm into *you*."

"I was afraid…" he began, but she silenced him with a kiss. She knew what he was going to say and it didn't matter, not now, not now that they were lovers.

"I bought breakfast food," she said, suddenly shy. "That is, unless you want to go out for breakfast, or unless I'm presuming too much?"

He propped himself up on one arm and smiled down at her. "Presume all you want to. You have no idea…"

"Oh, but I think I have."

GOOD NEIGHBORS

Jennifer Geneva

It was hot—a steamy Sunday night—and I couldn't sleep. I had just broken up with my boyfriend, Jason, and I missed the sex already. It was our only area of compatibility. We fought and had rough, angry, hot sex that kept us together. I tried calling him but his phone went straight to voice mail. I hung up without leaving a message, knowing he'd see I called.

School had just ended for the semester and my lifeguard job didn't start for another two weeks. I like working at the pool during the day but my favorite time is after the pool has closed and I'm the only one there. I take off my utilitarian red swimsuit and dive in, water stroking every inch of my skin, spreading my long, dark hair behind and around me. The swimming, the possibility of being caught and the warm air on my body usually turn me on so much I stretch out on a chaise lounge and rub my clit in just the right way until I come, biting my hand to avoid making the commotion that usually accompanies my orgasms.

I have a fantasy that gets me worked up and off every time.

I'm lying on the lounge, naked, starting my private workout. I run both hands up my body to my nipples, already erect and begging to be pinched and teased. I am startled by the sound of footsteps and open my eyes to find one of the water polo players who practices at the pool standing over me. His hard cock strains against the tight fabric of his Speedo. Without speaking, he peels it off.

I sit up, put my hand around the base of his gorgeous dick and pull on it gently. He moans. I flick my tongue around its head. He pulls my hair as my mouth takes his dick in farther. I roll my tongue around it, stopping periodically to give his balls some much-appreciated attention, and stop short when he looks like he's about to come.

I pull him onto the chair, on top of me. My legs are spread. He crawls between them and pulls them up over his shoulders. He shoves his huge cock into me and pumps me until he fills me to the edge of pain, staying on the right side. When he sees I'm about to come, he says, "Yeah," and we lose control at the same time.

As my body bucks and trembles, he disappears. When my fantasy ends, I jump in the pool to cool off and go home after another satisfying day at work.

Last night there was nothing to cool me down. My apartment doesn't have air-conditioning and my fan was no match for the humid June night.

I shed my tiny tank top and panties, trying to get more comfortable with a cold shower. When I got out, I stood in front of the fan, set at full blast. The heat made me cranky and my nakedness and the fan blowing cool air on my nipples made me horny.

I thought about getting myself off but I wanted to feel a real body up against mine. I wanted to sweat from more than just the hot night. I tried to distract myself: TV, reading, music. I called friends and got voice mail. I couldn't stop thinking about sex. I was pissed Jason had gotten over me so quickly.

Completely awake and frustrated, I went to the kitchen for a glass of water. I looked down at my body and thought of what a waste it was that no one was there to enjoy and excite me. With my long legs, tight ass, full tits with pink erect nipples, red toenails: it was a shame.

I guzzled the icy water, letting some cold droplets slide over my throat and nipples. I wished someone were there to lick the water from my skin. I poured myself another glass full. Looking out the large, uncovered window of my studio apartment, I saw a light on across the street. The blinds were open. I quickly forgot about the water. There was a woman standing right in front of a glass door, one hand alternately pinching each hard nipple, the other playing with her pussy. My mouth fell open.

She had long, dark hair and a luscious body, slick with sweat. We kind of looked alike, which was even hotter. A guy came up behind her, pressed up against her back and ass and grabbed her tits roughly. I imagined his hands on my nipples and shivered. He turned her around and pushed her up against the glass.

I had seen them before, coming and going from our apartments. Jason and I had noticed each other noticing them and talked about how hot it would be to have a foursome with them. We almost didn't make it inside before our clothes were off. He knew I had never fucked a girl and assumed the man was the subject of my fantasies. But this girl was sex on a stick and he would not have been more surprised than I was that I wanted to lick her like a Popsicle.

It was agonizing to watch without being a part of the fun, but I couldn't look away. She was on her knees now, his ass pressed against the door. I wanted to be him. I couldn't help touching myself. When they dimmed their lights, I had a better view of her body that was anything but boyish or lacking in any way. I watched her throw back her hair and tease him, playing with her alert nipples. I turned my own lights up, pulled out my vibrator, and hoped they would see me. I moved the vibrator around my outer lips, honing in slowly and deliberately toward my clit, teasing myself with a lower setting. After only a minute or so, I turned it up, thrust it in and out of my pussy a few times then concentrated the hard plastic on my pulsing clit. I came quickly and loudly. I didn't care about the neighbors near me. I just wanted my hot neighbors across the way to see me, especially her.

They were watching me and I loved it. I wasn't a theater major for nothing. Even audiences for *Our Town* got my juices flowing. What I hoped was the preview of *Our Threesome* was worthy of a standing O. Or a sitting O, or a lying on the floor, writhing O. They looked as turned on by my performance as I had been by theirs. They waved. I waved back. They gestured for me to come over. I didn't need to think. I pulled on my tank and a pair of very short shorts, grabbed my phone and keys and ran across the street.

The woman opened the door. Her naked body was glossy with sweat and her hair was damp, clinging to her face. She looked me up and down and slowly pulled off my tank top, then my shorts. Bypassing formal introductions, we kissed, pressing our hard nipples against each other. I had never kissed another woman; she instantly had me hooked.

The man was sexy as hell, with a huge cock and a clear knowledge of how to use it. I usually love that in a man, but I really wished he would leave. Go to the movies, to a bar, to the grocery store: frankly, I didn't care as long as he left. I wanted to explore her like an uncharted island, an ancient treasure chest, someone else's house.

The man reached around me and started massaging my wet clit with one hand while the other played with my nipples. He had long, thick, extremely capable fingers that quickly learned my body. I noticed the wedding band that matched hers and hoped I was this hot for my husband when I was married. I definitely hoped I'd be as adventurous. I pictured them together again and felt even more turned on, grinding my pussy hard against his hand.

He sat on a chair and pulled me onto him, hands on my hips directing the action. He pushed his hard cock into me again and again. I threw my head back, reveling in the sound of his balls slapping against me with every thrust. "Yeah, grind that hot pussy into me. Squeeze my cock with your tight little pussy. Yeah. Oh, fuck, yeah." He came like a shaken-up can of soda, the velocity almost knocking me to the floor. He held on to me but leaned back into the chair, snarling, head thrown back.

I'd had enough of him so I moved to another chair. She knelt down, met my eyes for a moment, then put her face between my legs, targeting my clit. Her tongue felt different from a man's, smaller and quicker, with a natural inclination to hit my sweet spot. She sucked and licked my now-aching clit, tasting his cum and my juices until I made my own animal sounds. We switched places. I used my own knowledge of the female body to eat her beautiful pussy, to explore her pink, sensitive folds and the hard nub of her swollen clit. Though I was a novice, I seemed to be a quick learner. I have always been good in school, head of the class. I saw gold stars in her eyes when she came, over and over. I was ready for more.

We were exhausted and sweaty. He got us glasses of cold water. We lay on the floor in front of the window, satiated but still caressing each other.

He broke the silence. "We're Rob and Jess," he said.

I smiled. "Lisa."

"We've seen you and your boyfriend. You always have your hands all over each other. We once watched you out the window while Rob took me from behind," Jess said.

I felt a sharp twinge between my thighs. Damn, this woman was pure sex.

"We broke up. That's why I was taking care of myself."

Rob and Jess looked at each other and laughed. Rob said, "You're welcome to join us anytime. Bring your ex, if you want." I knew this would thrill Jason. I also knew Jess worked from home—looked like something to do with clothing design. My plans to visit wouldn't always involve the boys—I had big plans for the dirty things we could do.

"I'll take you up on that but I should go now," I said, not wanting to overstay my welcome. "You guys wore me out." Beyond the smudged glass door, the sun was rising.

We stood. I looked out toward my apartment. Jess pressed herself against my back and Rob cupped her from behind. Through the pale shafts of daylight, we could see the silhouettes of several neighbors standing at their own windows. Half the block enjoyed the show. I was glad to have taken center stage. I kissed them both, pulled on my clothes and headed for the door.

"Come over for dinner tonight? Seven?" Jess looked she was already planning the recipes.

My phone vibrated: a text from Jason. *I want to fuck u.* I'm a sucker for the guy; the thought of him and Jess together made me shiver.

"It'll be for four. I'll bring dessert." I smiled and headed home to rest up for what was in store.

GIRL CRAZY

Gina de Vries

I am the girl who got run out of town because they worried about my influence. Something about their daughters and sons, my garter belt and stompy boots, my big mouth and piercing eyes. I am the girl who makes you nervous because I hold and keep your gaze when we're talking, when we're fucking. I am the girl who prefers your nervousness to your bravado, your hot desire to your cool aloofness.
— Girl Crazy #1, *Spider*

Okay, I realize that this is like Queer Girl Cliché number 573, but the first night I saw Spider was at a poetry reading her girlfriend organized at a feminist art gallery. I was twenty-one, spending my summer break from college doing an internship in San Francisco. I was fresh out of a miserable and controlling relationship and happy to be in a new and queer city. I was too naïve to realize I was fresh meat—the new girl in town who didn't realize how cute she was, who was caught off guard when

strangers flirted with her but also loved the attention. I was wide
eyed and green and into everything—especially sex. I was free
from my sourpuss possessive ex-girlfriend, and I wanted to play.
Like, all the time. Sex was all I thought about and all I wrote
about. Breakups and living in a new city full of possibilities will
make your hormones rage like nothing else, I swear to god.

> *I have been excess and lacking, too much and not
> enough all at once. I have been too slutty or too
> prudish, too fat or too skinny, too smart or not smart
> enough, too damaged or not broken down, too much
> like a boy or not enough of one. I am the queer, the
> whore, the freak, the geek. And whatever they might
> say about me, I know I have not failed.*
>   —Girl Crazy #1, *Spider*

I fucked more people that summer than I ever have before or
since. I kept a diary exclusively devoted to all the new people I
had in my bed, at parties, in alleyways, in the backseats of cars,
and once in the back room of a bar on a bar stool. It included
a lot of dreamy adjectives and adverbs—every detail I could
remember about these girls and boys and daddies and mommies.
What they wore, how they kissed, how big their cocks were, how
many cocks they had in the first place. Most of those folks, I'd
need to look back at that diary to even remember their names,
but Spider? Spider I *still* carry a torch for, after all these years
and with three thousand miles between us.

> *The kind of girls I like are sweet and mean and whip
> smart, lovely and vicious. They are bitch tops and
> bratty bottoms. They are fat girls with curves that
> wrap all the way around you and hold you up, hold*

you down, hold you. They are skinny girls with angles
so sharp they will cut anyone who dares to fuck with
the people they love.

—Girl Crazy #2, *Spider*

Is it cheesy to say I developed and kept the crush on her because
of her writing? I mean, also because of her bright shock of
blue-green hair and adorable fucked-up front teeth and septum
piercing juxtaposed with big Elvis Costello nerd glasses. Also
the fact that she rocked a men's blazer and skinny tie with plaid
pants and a fishnet shirt. Also the fact that her wheelchair was
covered in stickers from Queer Nation, and being from the
generation of queerness that came after Queer Nation, I just
thought that was the coolest thing imaginable.

But still it was mostly her writing. She read this poem the night
that I first saw her that just slayed me, opened me up to what
good honest writing could be. I was so hot, so intensely engaged,
that I came home that night, took out my journal, stayed up
writing till two, and then stayed up masturbating till three.

Most importantly, the girls I like are the kind of girls
whose femininity and queerness and very woman-
hood is hard-worn. Femmes get told a lot of lies in
life: You aren't strong. Real femmes don't act ballsy
and brassy and tough. Femmes are really straight
girls. Real dykes don't look like you. Real dykes
aren't whores. Real dykes aren't trans. Real dykes
don't have boyfriends. Real femmes need butches.
Real femmes aren't tops.

But I love the girls who do not believe the lies. I love
the girls who laugh in the faces of their deceivers.

—Girl Crazy #2, *Spider*

* * *

When I finally got up the nerve to talk with her at one of the open mics, she was so friendly—sweet and warm and she smiled at me so easy. She told me her name was Sal, and she asked me if I wanted a zine. I said of course I wanted a zine, and we just kept talking. We realized we'd both been riot grrrls at the same time—back when I was fourteen and she was twenty-two. "We might have been pen pals!" I said. "What was your zine called?"

"*Girl Crazy,* and I wrote under the name Spider."

"Wow," I said, "That sounds really familiar."

I went home that night and dug through the twenty zines I always packed with me no matter where I moved. Sure enough, there she was: A twenty-two-year-old disabled punk dyke who wrote beautiful and hilarious poetry under the pen name Spider Feminista. "God, I can't believe I almost legally changed my name to Spider Feminista when I was twenty-two!" She laughed when I called her up to confirm that we had, in fact, known each other when I was a teenager. "I'm glad people grow up. And I'm so glad you liked my zines. I need to find yours now, too, they have to be in my collection!"

I want to state for the record that I am glad that people grow up. I am for the most part annoyed by people who christen themselves things like Rex Anarchy and Octavian Sissypants. But I have to admit that I still think of her as Spider, still call her Spider in my head like it's a secret sweet pet name. It jarred me a little when people called her Sal. She will always be Spider to me, always that amazing girl who wrote those amazing zines.

This is not about narcissism. It is not about straight girls experimenting or "going wild" after one too many cocktails or joints, although one or both of us might have been straight, once. It is not about "taking a break" from boyfriends or husbands or the men we fuck, although one or both of us might fuck men sometimes, for fun or love or money or all three. It is about needing each other because we get each other. It is about being gorgeous, unbreakable, awe-inspiring together.

—Girl Crazy #3, *Spider*

Even after the weird and serendipitous zine moment, even after running into each other at countless readings and cafés and punk shows and her always asking how I was and always asking about my writing, I was shy. I was convinced she couldn't want me—because I was younger, because I was too nerdy, because I wore ballerina flats and sneakers with cats on them instead of Docs. She just seemed like the quintessential Tough Punk Dyke, and her girlfriend was smart and gorgeous with hair the color of summer roses, and purple fishnets, and the other lovers of hers I'd met were all spoken-word and zine superstars, and I was shy, not published anywhere except my zine.

And then she saw me read at an open mic, and I got the email the next day. I remember it to the letter. I can still recite it from memory:

Oh, pretty girl, I love the smut that you read at that open mic, about being sweet and submissive and hungry and dirty. I think you are so cute in your vintage dresses with your lovely curls and sparkly eyeliner. You are exactly the kind of girl I would love to take over my knee and spank with a hairbrush.

Also, if you wanted to come by my house and look at my books sometime, we could just do that, too. I

think you would very much enjoy my bookshelves.
                    —email from Spider, August 2004

Getting that email was like being struck by lighting: *She wants me. And she likes my writing.* Neither of those were small things when all I could think about was fucking her, when all I could do was read her work over and over till there were soft creases worn into the pages.

I had two weeks left in San Francisco before I went back to school in New York. We made plans to play that weekend. There was a big pansexual play party being thrown at the Fourteenth Street House—a giant purple Victorian between the Castro and Mission that was taken over by the Radical Fairies back in the '70s and repurposed for sex parties. It had three floors, with a serious S/M dungeon, a deck, a hot tub, and big rooms full of couches and giant pillows to fuck on. It was my first time at the house and maybe my second or third play party; I'm sure my mouth was hanging open for most of the night.

There wasn't an elevator or a ramp, so we got stuck on the ground level, doing an S/M scene around all the soft pillows and couches. It was a funny setting, but it made everything all the more surreal.

I didn't realize how much Spider got off on my youth and the fact that I was still in college until that night. She made good on her promise to take me over her knee and spank me with a hairbrush. I squirmed and yelped and she went on about how cute I was. But at some point during the spanking, she started talking about Foucault—asking me really intense questions about the panopticon and sex theory.

It occurred to me that she was pretending that she was an evil women's studies professor. I started to laugh, and couldn't stop. She talked a lot about "the importance of feminism awarding women sexual agency" while she hit me. The harder she hit me, the less control I had over my laughter. "Are you laughing at me?" she'd ask, and I'd nod, "Yes, I'm sorry! You're funny!" and then she'd hit me more, harder. She pulled my hair at strategic moments and asked me complicated questions about Andrea Dworkin. I'm sure I got some of them right, but that didn't really matter. Hitting was punishment for laughing and hitting was a reward for getting questions right, and I loved both.

She pulled her strap-on out of her tweed pants, rolled a condom onto her cock, and said, the corner of her mouth turned upward into a beautiful sneer, "I think feminism has empowered you enough to suck my dick." Ever since that night, I've been waiting for an opportunity to use that line on someone else.

She wouldn't even quit the professor talk when she fucked me. I remember her fingers, how she filled me slowly until almost her whole hand was inside me; nobody had gotten that much into me before. I remember telling her that between my moans, bracing my legs against the edge of the couch. I remember her murmuring back in time with her thrusts that I was a quick study, an apt pupil, a star student.

> *Our sex is not kittenish or tentative or soft. Our sex might be vulnerable, it might be complicated, it might even be awkward at moments. But do not mistake me for soft. Do not mistake laughing or crying or asking for it harder, lighter, faster, slower, with soft-focus lighting, with fake nails that you could never dream of slipping inside someone.*
> —Girl Crazy #3, *Spider*

We only played that one time. I came back to school and stayed on the East Coast, never lived in San Francisco again. I'm what feels like a million miles from Spider and San Francisco. She still sends me her zines and chapbooks, and I still read them and feel moved. Sometimes, when I'm feeling a little blue—lonely or unattractive or just sad about the state of the world—I pull out her zines. I read about girls and sex and possibility, and I smile to myself.

> *The kind of girls I like, they aren't nice girls either. Maybe they grew up in the city like I did, love the feel of the brick wall behind their backs in the alleyway, the feel of gravel under their knees; maybe they are small-town girls who knew all the secret places to chase skirt and cock and dreams back home; maybe they are country girls who know what it feels like to fuck under a sky blooming with stars.*
>
> *The kind of girls I like, they are brassy and street smart and wise and bold. They know what they want, and they never, ever apologize for asking for it.*

PSYCHOLOGY 101

R. Gay

Vanessa Vicente is one of the few professors at Markham University who commands perfect attendance throughout the semester. She's a striking woman—six feet tall, long red hair cascading down her back. Her blue eyes are wide and cat shaped. Her slender arms are perfectly sculpted—toned enough to make you look twice but not so muscular as to scare you. Her real prizes, though, are her breasts and her ass, both firm and round and crying out for the right lover's hands. Her mind is as amazing as her body. Vanessa's psychology lectures make the human psyche seem like the most fascinating and unknowable place in the world. Sometimes students are so busy listening to her delve into the mysteries of the cerebral cortex or the depths of human darkness they forget to take notes. She commands exorbitant fees on the lecture circuit. She's published seven books, two of which were *New York Times* best sellers. Vanessa Vicente is a rock star and she knows it.

She teaches in the main lecture hall on campus—the one that

holds nearly five hundred students. Every semester, the entire front row is populated by college boys and baby dykes wearing their baseball caps and dirty jeans, their Abercrombie T-shirts and flip-flops. They sit there, leaning forward, occasionally trying to wink at Vanessa or otherwise signal she has their full and undivided attention, reeking of boy and desperation. The futility of their efforts is nothing if not charming. I sit in the last seat of the front row, at the ready for anything Vanessa needs during class. I've been her teaching assistant for seven semesters now and I've gotten pretty good at giving her exactly what she needs.

Today, Vanessa is lecturing about brain chemicals and sexual impulses and more than one student is blushing or squirming in his seat but everyone is looking at Vanessa like she's the only thing that matters in the room. She's talking about how our ability to control our impulses is all about deferred gratification—we do it in the hope that waiting will get us those things we want. As I listen to the lecture I've heard several times before, my throat goes dry and by the end of class, my eyes are glassy. My thighs are tingling and I worry I might leave a wet spot on my seat.

After the last students trickle out of the lecture hall, Vanessa motions for me to join her at the lectern with the curl of a single slender finger. I gather my bag and my notepad and the voice recorder I use to record her lectures for later review and rush to her side. She rolls her eyes and plants a finger in the middle of my sweaty forehead. As I inch toward her, Vanessa smirks. Then she leans down and whispers a series of commands, her lips brushing against my earlobe, her breath cool against my neck. I nod and resist the urge to turn my head until our lips meet. Her lipstick smells sweet.

I was terrified of Vanessa when we first met. It was my first year as a PhD student and I didn't know much of anything and still, I was the envy of all my classmates. A position as Vanessa Vicente's graduate assistant was highly coveted. She met me in her office, which was large and filled with lots of natural light, shelves of books from floor to ceiling, a long leather couch against one wall. Vanessa sat in a Herman Miller chair wearing a sleeveless tunic and short skirt revealing a perfect pair of tanned, muscular thighs. As I stood in the doorway of her office wearing jeans and a frumpy blouse, I felt woefully underdressed. I leaned against the doorjamb, tried to control the trembling in my knees. Vanessa looked me up and down then shook her head. "You're going to be a lot of work, aren't you?" Her words were more declarative than interrogative.

A dark heat spread across my face. "No," I stammered, but she remained unconvinced.

"We're going to have to start with your wardrobe," Vanessa said. "I only like to look at pretty things." She wrote a few things on a notepad, tore the top page off, folded it in half and handed it to me along with a credit card. "Get everything on this list and be here at nine a.m. sharp, tomorrow." I nodded, eagerly clutching the paper between my sweaty fingers.

That was three and a half years ago. Since then, I've learned that Vanessa likes to look at a long neck, so I wear my hair swept up in a loose chignon. She likes to look at long legs, so I wear short skirts and high heels. She likes subtle scents so she chooses my perfumes. Vanessa expects me to work hard and be an outstanding scholar but she wants me to look good while doing it. Every time she makes a new, increasingly unreasonable request, I want her more and she knows it.

When we're in her office late at night, working, Vanessa will sit so close to me our arms are touching. She'll stare at my breasts then look into my eyes until I'm so uncomfortable I'm forced to look away. When she's feeling particularly cruel, she'll

slide a perfectly manicured hand between my knees and slowly
start inching her fingers up until she's reached the hem of my
skirt. I sit perfectly still but I always spread my legs apart until
we can smell and feel the heat of me.

If I try to touch her or kiss her thick, moist lips, she slides
away and returns her attention to her large computer monitor
as if nothing happened. Sometimes, when she's lecturing, I see
her watching me while she's talking about action potential
or catharsis or emotional intelligence. To everyone else she's
looking down at her notes or scanning the room but I know
better. When her eyes are on me, I lean forward and uncross
my legs, sometimes arching my back to give her a better view
of my breasts, hidden by clothes but framed by a silky black
bra chosen by her. Sometimes, I hold my coat on my lap and
when Vanessa Vicente is watching, I slide my hand under my
coat and beneath the waistband of my skirt. I bite my lower lip
and spread my swollen, slick pussy lips with two fingers. I start
stroking my clit, hard, hungry, hers. I breathe slow and shallow,
barely moving my fingers. When I do this, when I touch myself
while she's teaching, Vanessa grips the lectern so tightly I can see
the strain in her hands. I don't allow myself to come. I delay my
gratification. Then I smile at Vanessa and I trace my lips with my
wet fingers, tasting myself on my fingertips. When class is over,
I'll go to Vanessa to see what she needs and I'll touch her hand
and we'll both know I'm leaving a little bit of me with her.

After attending to Vanessa's requests, I meet her in her office.
She's shaking her hair out. She looks up. "What did you think of
today's lecture?" she asks.

I set my bag on the floor and lean against her desk. "Fascinating, as always. You did an excellent job of complicating the
notion of desire for the students."

Vanessa nods and smiles warmly. She sinks into her couch and sighs. "I've always known you were a smart girl. Most people think desire is a simple thing—they think we want therefore we must have. If I've taught you anything, it's that sometimes we have to want without being able to have."

I chuckle, thinking about our countless encounters of the unrequited kind. "I've definitely learned that."

I sit on the edge of Vanessa's desk and let my heels fall to the floor, twisting my ankles in lazy circles as the blood rushes back to my toes. After years of working together, we've developed a certain familiarity.

"What did you think about my discussion of how our ability to control our impulses is all about our faith in deferred gratification?"

I cross my legs and lean on one arm. Vanessa looks right into me and I hold her piercing gaze. "You handled that well though I do believe there is one thing you've neglected."

Vanessa smirks. "Just one thing?"

"Just one," I say.

She turns her hands upward. "Enlighten me."

I slide off her desk and close the short distance between us. I take a deep breath, then straddle her lap, clasping her wrists with my fingers. "You failed to discuss the reality that sometimes, we can't control ourselves." Before Vanessa can respond, I press my lips against hers, which are soft, full, inviting. A strange burning sensation begins to spread from beneath my breastbone outward and when she doesn't resist, I slide my tongue into the silky, salty warmth of her mouth. I kiss her greedily. She leans back into the cushions behind her and I hold her wrists over her head with one hand. With my other hand, I tear her blouse apart, squeezing her breast as I moan into her mouth.

Vanessa breaks free of my grip and stretches herself out along the length of her couch. She pats the empty space next to her.

I lie next to her on my side and drape one leg over hers. Vanessa pulls my lower lip between her teeth and slides a hand down my body, between my thighs and up my skirt. As she deftly pulls my panties aside, I close my eyes, inch closer. She grazes her thumb over my clit, just enough to make me whimper. I move closer still, nothing between us but our clothes.

Our lips meet again and I lift my leg high, inviting Vanessa inside me, where I want her, where I need her. She gently traces my pussy lips with her fingernails, a touch so soft it hurts. Suddenly, I feel like my clothes are strangling me. I sit up and shimmy out of my blouse and skirt, leaving my panties dangling around one ankle. I slide down to the floor and lie on my back. The only sound in the room is our husky, shallow breathing. I spread my legs wide. I bare myself to her. "Please," I beg. "Lose control with me."

Vanessa kneels between my open thighs. Her torn blouse slides off her shoulders revealing a perfectly even tan, everywhere. She leans down, kisses my neatly shaved mound, inhales deeply, then crawls up my body, her naked breasts and hard nipples leaving a train of goose bumps in their wake. As she lies alongside me, she begins rolling my nipples between her fingers, sweetly at first, then harder and harder until it feels like she is trying to squeeze through me. When she releases her grip, my nipples throb and she wraps her lips first around one, then the other, lathing them with her wide tongue. I gasp, spread my legs wider than I would have thought possible, rocking my hips even though there is nothing there.

"Don't make me wait any longer," I croak.

Vanessa pauses, then licks between my breasts, along the column of my throat to my chin. She traces my lips with her tongue then kisses me hard and sloppy, groaning as I respond eagerly. "I suppose," she finally says, "that the time for waiting has come and gone." With those words, years of sexual tension unravel from my spine and toward my limbs. She slides her hand down my body, her fingers splayed, and when she reaches my pussy, this time, she doesn't tease. She slides two fingers, then three into the heat and wetness of my cunt, buries herself deep inside me. Tears hover at the corners of my eyes. Vanessa straddles my naked thigh, hikes her skirt around her waist, revealing her beautiful pussy, covered in a pelt of fine red hair. As she thrusts her fingers inside me deeper, harder she begins grinding herself against my thigh, wetting my leg with her juices. Every stroke sends a sharp wave of pleasure through me. "More," I beg, and Vanessa fills me with a fourth finger, twisting her wrist from side to side, pressing at the doughy pad of membranes each time.

We have waited so long, have walked the tightrope of unspoken desire for so long, we come quickly, me holding her inside me as my body quakes around her, Vanessa riding me with a frenzied strength I have never known. When she pulls her hand away, I feel empty. I pull her fingers to my mouth, suckle each of them, tasting myself, tasting her, enjoying the sensation of her wetness drying on my thigh.

My mentor rolls onto her back next to me, our fingers and toes touching. As I try to catch my breath, I mumble, "That was me losing control."

Vanessa strokes my chin with her thumb and laughs. "It took you long enough," she says.

ABOUT THE
AUTHORS

KRIS ADAMS spends her days surrounded by words other people have written and her evenings surrounded by words of her own. She writes erotic and humorous fan fiction, in addition to original erotica. Her work can be found in *Best Women's Erotica 2009* and *Best Lesbian Romance 2010*.

CHEYENNE BLUE's erotica has previously appeared in multiple editions of *Mammoth Best New Erotica, Best Women's Erotica, Best Lesbian Love Stories, Best Lesbian Erotica, Best Lesbian Romance* and in *Foreign Affairs: Erotic Travel Tales, Rode Hard, Put Away Wet: Lesbian Cowboy Erotica, After Midnight: True Lesbian Erotic Confessions* and many other anthologies and websites.

RACHEL KRAMER BUSSEL (rachelkramerbussel.com) has edited over twenty-five anthologies, including *First-Timers, Glamour Girls, Dirty Girls, Spanked, Bottoms Up, The Mile High*

Club, Crossdressing and *Best Sex Writing 2008, 2009* and 2010. She writes about sex, books, and pop culture, is senior editor at *Penthouse Variations* and blogs at Cupcakes Take the Cake.

CARRIE CANNON has stories in *Best Women's Erotica 2010* and *Like a God's Kiss*. She's been paid to be a cookbook editor, a cook, a restaurant owner and a dog groomer, but writing smut is her favorite job so far.

ANGELA CAPERTON's eclectic erotica spans many genres to include romance, horror, fantasy, science fiction, contemporary, hard-edged noir and whimsical. Her erotic fantasy "Woman of the Mountain" won the 2008 Eppie for Best Erotica. Look for her stories published with Cleis Press, Black Lace, Circlet Press and eXtasy Books.

HEIDI CHAMPA's work appears in anthologies including *Tasting Him, Frenzy* and *Girl Fun One*. She has also steamed up the pages of *Bust* magazine. If you prefer your erotica in electronic form, she can be found at Clean Sheets, Ravenous Romance, Oysters and Chocolate and the Erotic Woman. Find her online at heidichampa.blogspot.com.

GINA DE VRIES's work has appeared in *Baby, Remember My Name: An Anthology of New Queer Girl Writing, Dirty Girls: Erotica for Women, TransForming Community, That's Revolting!: Queer Strategies for Resisting Assimilation, Bound to Struggle: Where Kink & Radical Politics Meet, make/shift* magazine and *Curve* magazine. She can be cruised online at ginadevries.com.

DELILAH DEVLIN creates dark, erotically charged paranormal worlds and richly descriptive westerns that ring with authenticity. Ms. Devlin has published over forty erotic romances. Visit her online at delilahdevlin.com.

DAVID ERLEWINE lives outside Annapolis with his wife and kids. He is a schlubby bureaucrat who likes writing smaller and smaller stories. His blog is whizbyfiction.blogspot.com.

GABRIELLE FOSTER lives and writes in London.

JENNIFER GENEVA is new to the world of erotica writing and hopes to visit again soon.

SHANNA GERMAIN's work may be found in places like *Best American Erotica, Best Bondage Erotica 2, Best Gay Bondage Erotica, Best Gay Erotica, Best Gay Romance, Best Lesbian Erotica, Dirty Girls, Frenzy, Playing with Fire* and at shannagermain.com.

MELISSA GIRA GRANT is a Brooklyn-based writer and sex worker rights advocate, whose work has recently appeared in *Slate, $pread*, BlackBook, Gawker, Valleywag, the *San Francisco Bay Guardian*, the Frisky, *Dirty Girls* (Seal Press), and *Best Sex Writing 2008* (Cleis Press). Her website is melissagira.com.

GENEVA KING (genevaking.com) has stories appearing in over a dozen anthologies including *Ultimate Lesbian Erotica 2009, Ultimate Undies, Caramel Flava* and *Travelrotica for Lesbians 1 & 2*. A transplant to Northern Maryland, she's constantly on the prowl for her next muse.

TERESA LAMAI is a novelist living in England. Her erotic stories have appeared in many anthologies, including *Best*

Women's Erotica, Best Lesbian Erotica, The Mammoth Book of Best New Erotica and Zane's *Caramel Flava*. She recently completed an anthology of dance-themed erotica titled *Swayed*.

ANNABETH LEONG is the alter ego of a technology journalist. Her erotica has appeared on the Oysters and Chocolate website and in *Experimental: an Anthology of Sex and Science*.

KIRSTY LOGAN is a writer (kirstylogan.com), editor, teacher, grad student, and general layabout. She lives in Scotland with her very own rebel girl.

EVAN MORA is a recovering corporate banker who's thrilled to put pen to paper after years of daydreaming in boardrooms. Her work can be found in *Best Lesbian Erotica '09, Best Lesbian Romance '09 & '10, Where the Girls Are, The Sweetest Kiss: Ravishing Vampire Erotica* and *Please, Sir*.

JULIA PETERS lives and works in New York City. Her fiction has been published in *Playgirl, The Mammoth Book of Best New Erotica, From Porn to Poetry 2* and others, as well as online at cleansheets.com, where she was a fiction editor. This is her first published work of erotica in quite some time.

G. G. ROYALE started writing erotica over ten years ago and has had several short stories published under different pen names. For the last three years, she has also worked as an editor for e-book publisher Loose Id, where she has helped polish over fifty manuscripts. Read more at ggroyale.blogspot.com.

LORI SELKE's fiction has appeared at Strange Horizons and Fishnet, and in anthologies such as *Homewrecker, Fucking*

*Daphne, Spicy Slipstream Stories*and *Bottoms Up*. Her writing also appears regularly in *Curve*. She lives in Oakland, California.

VANESSA VAUGHN's stories have been included in anthologies from Cleis Press, Circlet Press and Ravenous Romance. Vanessa is a bisexual author who loves edgy tales—especially those with lesbian or BDSM themes. For more on her current projects, please visit her blog at VanessaVaughn.com.

ABOUT THE EDITOR

R. GAY's writing appears in numerous anthologies and magazines including *Best American Erotica 2004* and *Best Women's Erotica 2008*. Visit her online at pettyfictions.com.